SECRET THOUGHTS

D0756756

Also by David Lodge

SECRET THOUGHTS

A play for two actors
Based on the novel *Thinks* . . .

David Lodge

Harvill Secker
LONDON

Published by Harvill Secker 2011

2 4 6 8 10 9 7 5 3 1

Copyright © David Lodge 2011

David Lodge has asserted his right under the Copyright, Designs and Patents Act 1988 to
be identified as the author of this work

This book is sold subject to the condition that it shall not, by way of trade or otherwise,
be lent, resold, hired out, or otherwise circulated without the publisher's prior consent in
any form of binding or cover other than that in which it is published and without a similar
condition including this condition being imposed on the subsequent purchaser

First published in Great Britain in 2011 by
HARVILL SECKER
Random House
20 Vauxhall Bridge Road
London SW1V 2SA

www.randomhouse.co.uk

Addresses for companies within The Random House Group Limited can be found at:
www.randomhouse.co.uk/offices.htm

The Random House Group Limited Reg. No. 954009

A CIP catalogue record for this book is available from the British Library

ISBN 9781846555534

All rights whatsoever in this play are strictly reserved. Requests to reproduce the text in
whole or in part should be addressed to the publishers. Application for performance in
any medium or for translation in any language should be addressed to the author's agents:
in respect of performance rights to The Agency Ltd, 24 Pottery Lane, London W11 4LZ;
in respect of translation rights to Curtis Brown Group Ltd, 4th Floor, Haymarket House,
28/29 Haymarket, London SW1Y 4SP

The Random House Group Limited supports The Forest Stewardship
Council (FSC), the leading international forest certification organisation. All our titles
that are printed on Greenpeace approved FSC certified paper carry the FSC logo. Our
paper procurement policy can be found at
www.randomhouse.co.uk/environment

Mixed Sources
Product group from well-managed
forests and other controlled sources
www.fsc.org Cert no. TT-COC-2139
© 1996 Forest Stewardship Council
FSC

Typeset by Palimpsest Book Production Limited,
Falkirk, Stirlingshire
Printed and bound in Great Britain by
CPI Bookmarque Ltd, Croydon, Surrey

Secret Thoughts was first performed at the Bolton Octagon Theatre on 13th May 2011. It was directed by David Thacker. His Assistant Director was Elizabeth Newman. The designer and lighting designer was Ciaran Bagnall. The cast was as follows:

HELEN REED   Kate Coogan
RALPH MESSENGER   Rob Edwards

★

I am indebted to Benoît Verhaert for the idea of adapting my novel, *Thinks* . . . as a play for two actors. How this happened is explained in the Foreword. *Secret Thoughts* was performed at the Octagon Theatre on a thrust stage, with minimal props, using music and lighting to mark shifts in time and space. It could, however, be presented on a proscenium stage, and with a more realistic set. To allow for a variety of production styles the stage directions in this text are also minimal. As it went to press before the end of rehearsals there may be some small differences from the play as performed.

D.L.

FOREWORD

I can recall exactly the occasion when I had the first glimmering of an idea for the novel eventually published in 2001 as *Thinks . . .* It was reading in the Catholic weekly, *The Tablet*, in June 1994, a review by John Cornwell of two books – Daniel Dennett's *Consciousness Explained* and Francis Crick's *The Astonishing Hypothesis*. The review was headed 'From Soul to Software' and it interested me very much. First, it was news to me that consciousness had become a hot topic of enquiry for scientists in many different fields. Second, I was struck by Cornwell's exposition of the challenge that the arguments of Crick and Dennett presented to traditional religious and humanist ideas of the individual self or soul. Crick's hypothesis, to which Dennett would subscribe, is that '"You", your joys and your sorrows, your memories and your ambitions, your sense of personal identity and free will, are in fact no more than the behaviours of a vast assembly of nerve cells and their associated molecules.' I had a hunch that there might be a novel in this subject, of the kind in which a conflict between two opposed cultures or value systems is explored in a human story.

But first I had to familiarise myself with the research and arguments going on in the field of 'consciousness studies', which embraces neuroscience, artificial intelligence, zoology, psychology, philosophy and many other disciplines, and is infused with the neo-Darwinian evolutionary biology disseminated by popular science writers like Richard Dawkins. This was a considerable task for someone who had 'dropped' science subjects at school as soon as he could. It was educative but time-consuming, and some years passed before I began writing a novel about Ralph Messenger, a cognitive scientist specialising in artificial intelligence, and Helen Reed, a novelist in her early forties who is still grieving for her husband who died suddenly a year before. She comes as a visiting teacher of creative writing to a university where Ralph, an incorrigible womaniser, is director of a prestigious research institute, and attracts his attention. They argue about the nature of consciousness and related issues while she struggles to resist his sexual advances. He is an atheist and philosophically a materialist; she is a Catholic who has lost her faith but still yearns for the consolations of religion.

Early in their acquaintance Ralph explains that the problem

for scientists studying consciousness is that it is 'a first-person phenomenon' experienced by a subjective 'I', but science is an objective, third-person discourse. How can the former be described by the latter? Helen says that novelists have been doing this successfully for nearly two hundred years, by the technique of 'free indirect style' which allows the novelist to combine the inner voice of a character and the voice of a narrator, and she reads Ralph a passage from Henry James to prove her point. Ralph retorts that in real life, unlike fiction, 'We can never know for certain what another person is thinking.' I decided to tell their story from three points of view, two subjective and one objective. Ralph is dictating his random thoughts into a tape recorder to provide data for his research; Helen is writing a diary on her laptop. These discourses describe their developing relationship and alternate with another, impersonal, objective, third-person account of the same events, which is restricted to reporting what they say and do, without describing their thoughts and feelings. Interpretation of these three parallel narratives is left to the reader without authorial guidance.

In the course of my twin career as a university teacher of literature and creative writer I became increasingly interested in the theory and practice of adaptation, especially in the question of what is gained and what is lost in the process. Narrative is a universal feature of all human culture, and in principle is translatable from one language to another and from one medium to another. The story of *Cinderella* can be told orally or in print, in English or French, as a pantomime or a ballet, a film or a strip cartoon, and still have essentially the same meaning in all these realisations. But more complex and sophisticated narratives are not so easily adaptable. Stage plays have to be 'opened out' when they are made into films or risk seeming artificial, but often lose some of their intensity in the process. Novels tend to contain too much plot and too many characters to be satisfactorily dramatised within the constraints of theatrical time and resources: an entertaining show may result, but much of the quality of the original is lost. Film is a more compatible medium for the adaptation of a novel, because both forms move their stories through time and space in much the same way, and the TV serial is better still, because it gives room to unfold a long and complex story.

Both stage play and film or TV drama can bring a thrilling new dimension to a novel by the physical presence and performance of the actors, but – restricted to showing what can be seen and heard – all these media struggle to do justice to the representation of consciousness, which is silent and invisible. I enjoyed some success, and derived great satisfaction, from adapting my novel *Nice Work* and Dickens's *Martin Chuzzlewit* as TV serials, greatly helped by the fact that in both novels the story unfolds in dramatic encounters and confrontations between the characters, rather than in their minds. The 'stream-of-consciousness' novel – Virginia Woolf's, for example – is the kind of fiction most resistant to cinematic treatment. Using 'voice-over' in film to articulate the silent thoughts of characters must be used sparingly, if at all, because it goes against the grain of the medium – at least that is the orthodox view, or prejudice, in the Anglo-American film industry. Continental European film-makers are more comfortable with this device, and have had considerable success with it. I spent some time in the late 1990s developing a film script of my novel *Therapy*, much of it in collaboration with the director David Thacker, who had suspended his distinguished career in the theatre to work in TV and film; and later we pitched *Thinks . . .* to the BBC as a possible TV serial. Neither project came to fruition, but if they had, 'voice-over' would have been essential, especially with *Thinks . . .*

Late in 2006 I received a letter from a Belgian director/actor/writer, Benoît Verhaert, previously unknown to me, asking for permission to adapt *Thinks . . .* as a play for two actors, based on the French translation, *Pensées Secrètes*, for production at Théâtre le Public, a small but prestigious subsidised theatre in Brussels. He enclosed a rough, incomplete draft of his proposed play. It had never previously occurred to me that this novel could be adapted for the stage. The relationship of Ralph Messenger and Helen Reed is embedded in a particular social context – a 'greenfield' university of 1960s vintage, with its students and faculty, several of whom are important characters in the way the story develops. Ralph's relationship with his wife Carrie and the backstory of Helen's deceased husband are significant elements in the complex plot, which extends over several months. It would be impossible to incorporate all these characters and events in a stage play for both practical and dramaturgical reasons. But Benoit's proposal suddenly made me realise that one could tell the essential story of the relationship between Ralph Messenger and Helen Reed, and explore the moral, philosophical and intellectual issues it involves, without all the dense contextual material of the novel. That could be stripped away without affecting the coherence of the central narrative, which could unfold through monologues based on Ralph's tape recordings and Helen's diary entries, alternating with scenes of dialogue between them, of which there are many in the 'third-person' sections of the novel. There would be no need to have any other characters. The conventions of stage drama, which require the audience to accept a degree of overt artifice in the presentation of experience, would make this stylised version of the novel viable. And it might provide parts with which two actors could create something memorable.

So I reasoned as I considered Benoît's proposal, and immediately I was seized with a desire to attempt such an adaptation myself. Accordingly, I gave him permission to proceed with his French-language version, but reserved the right to do any adaptation in English myself. I looked forward to seeing how his play worked on the stage before I started writing my own, and in the meantime I read and commented on his draft script. Benoît explained to me that his practice in adapting novels for the stage (of which he had considerable experience) was to restrict himself to using the actual words of the author, but not necessarily in the same order. I was surprised, however, to find that he began his play with the talk about consciousness that Helen gives to a cognitive science conference, at Ralph's invitation, near the end of my novel. In Benoît's version Ralph introduces her to the audience, who stand in for the imaginary conferees. The narrative implication is that she has been teaching on the campus for some weeks, but they have only just met, and their relationship develops from that point. This was a neat way to establish the identity of the two characters and the context of consciousness studies at the beginning of the play, but I saw difficulties in using Helen's talk, as written, in that position in the story. I would have to wait and see how it, and other quite radical rearrangements of the components of my novel, worked on the stage.

In September 2007 I went to Brussels with my wife Mary to attend the first night of *Pensées Secrètes*. Théâtre le Public is a comfortable and well-equipped building which looks on the outside as if it was once an old warehouse, with three acting spaces, of which the largest has only 300-odd seats – just right for a play of this kind. The artistic director, Michel Kacenelenbogen, is an actor, and had chosen to play the part of Ralph himself, with his wife, Patricia Ide, as Helen. He told me when we met in his office in the afternoon before the performance that it was, surprisingly, the first time they had ever acted together. I said I was honoured. He certainly looked the part – a big, genial, extrovert man – and Patricia Ide, when we met, seemed perfect casting for Helen.

So it proved in performance, but as I had anticipated, her talk, which opposes the literary humanist's view of consciousness to the scientific approach, did not fit easily into its new position in the story. Patricia impersonated very well an arts-educated writer's nervousness at addressing an audience of scientists; but the talk is in fact a very articulate synthesis of what, in the novel, she (and vicariously the reader) have learned about the subject of consciousness in the course of many arguments with Ralph. It was quite a challenging long speech to throw at the audience at the very beginning of the play, and for the first twenty minutes or so they kept what seemed to me a somewhat baffled silence. But gradually they began to grasp what the play was about, to laugh at the jokes, and respond to the twists in the story. The piece was beautifully designed and lit, and imaginatively directed. At the end (it was played without an interval) the audience applauded warmly. It was a successful evening, and the play had good audiences for its allotted run of eight weeks and, with one exception, favourable reviews. But it was not the play I had in my head – which was in fact a relief to me. I told Benoît that I intended to have a go at doing my own adaptation and that, if anything came of it, I would ensure that he received a percentage of the royalties, because the original idea of doing the play as a two-hander was his, and I would never have thought of it myself. However, I intended to follow the sequence of events and the emotional arc of the novel more faithfully than he did, and in consequence my play turned out to be very different from his, apart from the words taken from their common source, the original novel.

It also acquired quite a lot of new words, especially after David Thacker, who had returned to work in theatre as artistic director of the Bolton Octagon in 2009, offered to put it on there. At my first meeting to discuss the play with him and his assistant director, Elizabeth Newman, they pointed out that the script, based on a novel written more than ten years ago, needed bringing up to date if it was supposed to be set in the present day, particularly with reference to communications. It would hardly be credible, for instance, that Helen would come to teach at the university today without email installed on her laptop, as she does in the novel. My microbiologist daughter and computer-savvy son-in-law read the play and helped me modify the practical assistance Ralph gives to Helen in this respect, and also to update his expositions of evolutionary biology. The name of the fictitious University of Gloucester had to be changed because the University of Gloucestershire has been created since I wrote the novel. (I moved it to Harrogate.) And more importantly, in two day-long sessions, with David and Elizabeth reading the two parts, we tested every line of the play for coherence, plausibility and dramatic relevance, and I made notes for cuts and rewrites, until we eventually had a script we were all happy with.

It was an absorbing and satisfying experience, but there is no way of knowing whether a play 'works' until, after much collaborative effort by director, actors, designers and auxiliary staff, it is performed in the presence of an audience. The process that will bring that about for *Secret Thoughts* has barely begun as I write this. Putting on a play is itself a collective drama, generating for the participants at different times hope, frustration, euphoria, disappointment and many other emotions. It has no equivalent in the solitary experience, intensely anxious as it often is, of writing a novel and seeing it through to publication. And if you are wondering why I want to bother converting a successful novel into another form and encountering a whole set of new problems in the process, the answer is this: it is not easy to invent a good story, and when you think you have one it is hard to resist the impulse to explore its possible meanings further, and to attract new audiences to it, by translating it into another medium.

D.L., January 2011

ACT ONE

Two areas of the stage have essential items of furniture. To one side: the living room of a small modern flat, with a table that serves as a desk, a small printer on or beside it, one upright chair for the desk, a small armchair with a coffee table beside it. There are ways out, one leading to a bedroom and another leading to the kitchen/bathroom/entrance hall, which are unseen. On the other side of the stage, an office in a hi-tech university institute, a desk with a PC and flat screen on it, a printer, a tilting swivel chair, an upright chair and a place to hang coats. Telephones on both desks.

Scene One

A winter evening. HELEN REED, *an attractive woman in her early forties, sits at a table in her flat, typing on a laptop. She stops typing and reads aloud what she has just written. After reading a few sentences she looks up from the screen of the laptop while continuing to speak. It is implied that these words are a continuation of her thoughts, a mental draft of what she intends to write next. At the end of the speech she resumes typing. (There may be other ways of performing* HELEN*'s monologues but it is important to establish that she is recording her thoughts in a journal on her laptop. In the course of the monologues she might move from the desk, but she normally returns to the desk at the end of them.)*

HELEN

Thursday evening, the seventeenth of February. Well, here I am, settled in, more or less. I've been allocated a little flat on the campus, reserved for visiting teachers. An open-plan living room with kitchenette . . . and a bedroomette and a bathroomette. It's quite big enough for me, actually, but I must say I miss the spacious rooms and high-corniced ceilings of home. Home! I must stop thinking about home.

Act One Scene One

This is my home for the next fifteen weeks, the
spring semester. I saw my name in the arts faculty
handbook today: '*MA in Creative Writing. Prose
Narrative. Tuesdays and Thursdays, 2–4 p.m. Tutor:
Helen Reed.*' It felt like the confirmation of a jail
sentence . . . In fact, Harrogate University *is* a bit
like a very nicely landscaped open prison. It's one
of those universities built in the 1960s, on greenfield
sites outside cathedral cities and towns of character.
They were called 'the new universities' then, but this
one is already showing its age, the concrete and tiles
haven't weathered well – except for a building made
of stainless steel and mirror glass, with a domed roof
divided down the middle, an Institute of Cognitive
Science, I'm told. Whatever that is . . .

I haven't met my students yet – classes don't begin
until next week. Perhaps I'll feel more cheerful
once I get started. I hope so – that was the whole
point of taking this job. In the meantime my only
prospect of society is a dinner party on Saturday,
hosted by the Vice Chancellor, to welcome new
members of staff – a professor of metallurgy and
me, a combination which may present a
conversational challenge.

It seems to get dark earlier here than it does at
home – there I go again! Of course it's never really
dark in London – all those millions of street lamps
. . . It's eerily quiet, too, after five o'clock, when
the faculty drive off to their homes in Harrogate or
the local villages. I can actually hear the sound of
single vehicles on the road beyond the perimeter
fence. (*Pause.*) God, I feel wretched.

Coming here was a terrible mistake, I want to run
away, I want to scuttle back home to London.
Leave a note saying, '*Sorry, I made a mistake, all my
fault, please forgive me.*' But I can't. I must do my
time. (*She resumes typing.*)

Music.

2

Scene Two

Morning. Professor RALPH MESSENGER, *a handsome man in his fifties, is alone in his office in the Institute of Cognitive Science, of which he is Director, on the campus of the University of Harrogate. He is a self-confident man, both intelligent and sensual. He is casually dressed. He sits by his desk in a chair that tilts and swivels, and holds a pocket micro-cassette voice recorder in his hand.*

> RALPH
>
> One, two, three, testing, testing . . . (*He plays back these words.*) Recorder working OK . . . It's a bit of an antique now . . . I bought it at Heathrow in the duty-free on my way to . . . where? Can't remember, doesn't matter . . . The object of the exercise being to record as accurately as possible the thoughts that are passing through my head at this moment in time, which is, let's see . . . (*glances at watch*) 9.53 a.m., on Sunday the 20th of Febru— San Diego! I bought it on my way to that conference in San Diego, 'Vision and the Brain'. Of course – Isabel Hennessey. She gave a paper on 'Modelling Three-dimensional Objects'. I tested the range of the condenser mike . . . (*hesitates*) Yes . . . Where was I? But that's the point, I'm not anywhere, I haven't made a decision to think about anything specific, the object of the exercise being simply to record the random thoughts passing through a man's head, all right, my head, at a randomly chosen time and place . . . well, not truly random, I came into the Institute on purpose knowing it would be deserted on a Sunday morning, I wouldn't be interrupted, distracted, overheard, nobody else around . . . The object of the exercise being to try and describe the structure of, or rather to produce a specimen, that's to say raw data, on the basis of which one might begin to try to describe the structure of, or from which one might *infer* the structure of . . . thought.

Pause.

Act One Scene Two

Lights down on RALPH*'s office. He remains seated, thinking.*

Lights up on HELEN*'s flat. She is seated at the table, typing on the laptop. She begins to speak, at first reading from the screen and then uttering her thoughts aloud, as in Scene One.*

HELEN

Sunday morning, the twenty-first of February. Yesterday evening's dinner party was less of an ordeal than I had feared. There was just one sticky moment during the pre-dinner drinks when the Vice Chancellor's wife complimented me on writing one of Margaret Drabble's novels. I didn't like to correct her publicly. Luckily one of the other guests, Carrie Messenger, spotted the mistake and deftly changed the subject. She's the wife of Ralph Messenger, who's Director of that strange-looking building, the Cognitive Science Institute, and something of a star here. I knew his name as a reviewer of science books in the Sunday papers, and I saw him once on television. He was standing in front of some machine, a brain-scanner I think, and saying to camera: '*So is happiness – or unhappiness – just a matter of the hard-wiring in your brain?*'

Lights down on HELEN.

Lights up on RALPH. *He resumes dictation.*

RALPH

Is consciousness like a stream, as William James said? Or, as he also rather beautifully said, like a bird flying through the air and then perching for a moment, then taking wing again, flight punctuated by moments of – Incidentally, how is the audiotypist going to punctuate *this*? I'll have to give instructions – say, put dots for a short pause, and a full stop for a longer pause. (*looks at recorder*) Nifty little gadget . . . Isabel Hennessey . . . I recorded us in bed to test the range of the condenser mike, left it running on the chair with my clothes without her knowing . . . She made a lot of noise when she came. I like that in a woman . . . Carrie won't unless we're

4

alone in the house, which doesn't happen very
– Jesus Christ! I can't have this stuff transcribed!
Even if I send it to an agency there's always a risk
somebody would recognise the names and send it
to *Private Eye,* or even try to blackmail me, fuck,
and I can't change the names as I go along, be too
difficult, too distracting, I'll have to transcribe the
bloody thing myself, fuck, what a bind. I should
have thought of that . . . But then I only got the
idea this morning in bed, lying awake in the dark, I
didn't sleep well, a touch of indigestion, I didn't
really like that starter at the VC's dinner party, crab
mousse or whatever it was . . . Where was I?

Lights down on RALPH.

Lights up on HELEN. *She is still musing over her laptop.*

HELEN
It was interesting to meet him in the flesh. He's
friendly, clever, amusing, but a bit vain, a bit arrogant.
His wife calls him 'Messenger' which has a curious
effect, half deferential, half ironic. She's American,
and rich, I gather, so they live in a style above the
standard of the average professor, with a listed house
in Harrogate and a weekend cottage in the Dales. She
must have been a real beauty when she was young,
but, as she disarmingly confessed to me, lost the
battle against cellulite between her second and third
babies . . . She's still lovely, though . . . They make a
handsome couple. I watched them leave the house with
a pang of envy, walking across the gravel drive to their
big Mercedes, his arm round her shoulder. Couples
can still have that effect on me, even a year after Martin
. . . (*tears welling*) I thought I'd stopped that.

She closes down the laptop, gets up, and goes out to the hall.
Lights down on HELEN's *flat.*

Scene Three

Lights up on RALPH, *who continues to dictate.*

RALPH

Where was I? You don't have to be anywhere,
remember. But it was something interesting . . .
Isabel Hennessey . . . no, not her . . . not that she
was uninteresting . . . What a lot of pubic hair she
had, black and springy and densely woven, like a
birds' nest . . . James! Yes, William James, and his
idea of consciousness as a bird, flying and perching
. . . The interesting question is, are those perchings
of the bird completions of a thought or pauses in
thought, blanks, white space? White noise would be
better because there is brain activity still going on all
the time or you would be dead . . . '*I think therefore
I am*' is true enough in that sense . . . Must be the
best-known sentence in the history of philosophy.
What's the second best-known? I wonder . . . But
is thought continuous, inescapable, or is it, as
somebody said against Descartes, '*Sometimes I think
and sometimes I just am* . . .'? Can I just am without
thinking?

Of course, this experiment is hopelessly artificial
because the decision to record one's thoughts is
bound to influence the thoughts one has . . . For
instance, I feel a little stiffness in my neck at this
moment, I move my head, I stretch . . . I swivel
round in my chair . . . I get up . . . I walk from
my desk to the window . . . (*He does so, and looks
out of a window.*) All these things I would normally
do without thinking, I would do them
'unconsciously' as we say, but this morning I'm
conscious of them because I hold a tape recorder in
my hand, specifically for the purpose of –

HELEN, *in raincoat and headscarf, enters, stops, looks around.*

RALPH

Who is that wandering about the campus on a wet
Sunday morning? She doesn't look as if she's going
anywhere, just going for a walk, but who'd go for a
walk in this drizzle? Oh, it's that woman at the dinner

party last night, the writer, she's taking over Russell Marsden's course while he's on study leave, Helen Somebody . . . Helen Reed, yes of course, she's living on campus in one of those flats on the west perimeter, she told me before dinner, she's let her own house for the semester. 'So you won't be nipping back to London from Thursday evening to Tuesday morning like most of our visiting writers,' I said. 'No,' she said, 'I've burned my boats, or is it bridges?' and smiled, but there was a sad look in her eyes as she said it, nice eyes, very dark brown irises, attractive woman altogether . . . And then dinner was served and I didn't have another chance to speak to her, we were at opposite ends of the table . . . Carrie sat next to her and said she was very nice . . . Apparently her husband died suddenly about a year ago . . . There she goes, round the corner of Biology. Wonder where she's going, what she's doing, at ten fifteen on a wet Sunday morning, must be lonely as hell living here on her own . . . I could go after her now, pretend to bump into her, or say 'I just happened to see you from my office window, we didn't really have much chance to talk yesterday evening . . .' Why not?

He switches off the recorder, grabs his coat and goes out. HELEN *goes off.*

Scene Four

The campus. RALPH *looks around, puzzled. In the distance faintly the sound of a Catholic hymn being sung by a congregation.* RALPH*'s mobile rings. He takes it from his pocket.*

RALPH
Messenger. Oh, hi. Yes, fairly soon . . . Milk? OK, I'll get some at a garage on the way home . . . Yes, there does seem to be some singing coming from somewhere – it must be our ecumenical faith centre, all superstitions welcome . . . Well, I just popped out for a breath of air . . . What's for lunch? . . . Then I certainly

won't be late . . . What? . . . Oh. (*disappointed*) I was hoping the kids would amuse *themselves* this afternoon, and we could have a little siesta . . . Because you are my wife, Carrie, and I desire you . . . And because you didn't want to last night. Then I can't rest until I've had you, even after all these years . . . (*Carrie evidently terminates the call. He addresses the phone.*) Well, that's life, Carrie. Or men. Or me.

Music.

Scene Five

The campus. A sunny winter morning. HELEN, *wearing her raincoat unbuttoned, is sitting on a bench reading a small hardback book.* RALPH, *passing, notices her.*

RALPH
Hello.

HELEN
Oh, hello.

RALPH (*goes over to her*)
Enjoying the sun?

HELEN
It's amazingly warm for the time of year.

RALPH
How are you settling in?

HELEN
All right.

RALPH
Only all right?

HELEN
I haven't started teaching yet – I expect then I'll feel less . . .

RALPH
Lonely?

HELEN

Well . . . marooned.

RALPH

Actually I saw you wandering about in the rain
yesterday morning, looking a bit lost.

HELEN (*disconcerted*)

How did you see me?

RALPH

From my office window.

HELEN

Do you work on Sundays, then?

RALPH

Er . . . sometimes. I went out to look for you, I
was going to offer you a cup of coffee, but you'd
disappeared into thin air.

HELEN

I was in the chapel.

RALPH

The chapel?

HELEN

I went in to shelter from the rain.

RALPH

Oh good.

HELEN

Why 'good'?

RALPH

I was afraid you might have had a religious motive.
It's impossible to have a serious conversation with
religious people – or an amusing one for that matter.

HELEN

I was brought up as a Catholic, and I recognised the
hymn they were singing in the chapel, so I went in
and sat at the back and heard the rest of the Mass.

9

RALPH
But you're not a believer?

HELEN
I don't believe in the doctrine any more, but
sometimes I think there must be a kind of truth
behind it. Or I hope there is.

RALPH
Why?

HELEN
Because otherwise life seems pointless, ultimately.

RALPH
I don't find it so. I find it full of interest and deeply
satisfying. Why d'you need religion?

HELEN
I don't *need* it exactly, but there are times . . . I lost
my husband, you see, about a year ago.

RALPH
Yes, I heard about that.

HELEN *seems to expect some commiseration, but it doesn't come.*

HELEN
It was very sudden, an aneurysm in the brain. Our
lives were going so well when it happened. I'd just
won a prize, and Martin had just been promoted, we
were looking through holiday brochures when . . .
(*on the verge of tears*) when he just collapsed. He went
into a coma and died the next day in hospital.

RALPH
That must have been tough for you . . . But for him it
was a good way to go.

HELEN (*shocked*)
How can you say that? He was only forty-four. He
had years of happy life to look forward to.

RALPH
Who knows? He might have developed some horribly
painful degenerative disease next year.

HELEN
And he might not.

RALPH
No, he might not.

HELEN
He might have made lots more brilliant radio
documentaries and gone round the world and had
grandchildren and . . . all kinds of things.

RALPH
But he didn't have time to think about that before
he died. He died full of hope. The pain of loss is all
yours.

Pause.

HELEN
So you think that when we die we just cease to
exist?

RALPH
Not in an absolute sense. The atoms of my body are
indestructible.

HELEN
But your self, your spirit, your soul . . . ?

RALPH
As far as I'm concerned those are just fictions
produced by certain kinds of brain activity. When the
brain ceases to function, they cease too.

HELEN
And that doesn't fill you with despair?

RALPH
No, why should it?

HELEN
Well, it seems so pointless to spend years and years
acquiring knowledge, accumulating experience, trying
to *make* something of yourself, as the saying goes, if
nothing of that self survives death.

RALPH

I hope to leave a permanent mark on cognitive science before I go, just as you must hope to do in literature. That's a kind of life after death. The only kind.

HELEN

Cognitive science . . . what is it, exactly?

RALPH

The systematic study of consciousness.

HELEN

Oh, that.

RALPH

You know about it?

HELEN

Vaguely. I've noticed a lot of books being published with that word in the title. I haven't read any of them, I'm afraid.

RALPH

There are a lot of books because all kinds of people are into consciousness these days – neurologists, psychologists, biologists, even physicists . . .

HELEN

Which of those are you?

RALPH

None. I started out as a philosopher. Then I moved into AI. Once upon a time –

HELEN

AI?

RALPH

Artificial intelligence. Once only philosophers were interested in the problem of consciousness. Now it's the biggest game in town.

HELEN

What's the problem?

RALPH

Well, it's the old mind–body conundrum: how

does a physical brain produce the mental phenomenon of consciousness? Don't you ever ask yourself that?

HELEN

I can't say I do. I'm more interested in the contents of my mind . . . emotions, sensations, feelings.

RALPH

They're part of the problem. We call them *qualia* in the trade.

HELEN

Qualia?

RALPH

The specific quality of our subjective experiences of the world. Like the smell of coffee, or the blue of the sky on a clear day . . . or the feel of a kiss. They're impossible to describe scientifically. Nobody's proved they actually exist.

HELEN

There's no need to! They *are* the proof.

RALPH

Well, they *seem* real enough to us, individually, while they're happening, but they can't be observed by anyone else. They're intangible effects produced by events in the hard-wiring of our brains.

HELEN

Like happiness and unhappiness?

RALPH (*pleased*)

You saw my TV series?

HELEN

Only a bit of it. And that was by accident. (*apologetically*) I don't watch science programmes as a rule.

RALPH

Well, I don't go all the way with the neuroscientists. The mind is a machine, yes, but a *virtual* machine.

It's like a computer. You write on a computer, I
presume?

HELEN

I've got a laptop. I've no idea how it works.

RALPH

OK. Your laptop runs different programs
simultaneously so that you can switch from one to
another – word processing, Internet searches, email
– and cut and paste between them. The brain is
like an infinitely more complex parallel computer,
running an enormous number of programs at terrific
speed. The possible interactions between them are so
complex that it's very difficult to simulate the process
– but we're getting there, as British Rail used to say.

HELEN

You mean, at your Institute, you're trying to design a
computer that thinks like a human being?

RALPH

That's the ultimate objective, yes.

HELEN

And feels like a human being? A computer that feels
pain, and falls in love, and suffers bereavement?

RALPH

Pain might be difficult – it depends how you define it.
But it would be quite possible to design a robot that
could get into a symbiotic relationship with another
robot and would exhibit symptoms of distress if the
other robot were put out of commission.

HELEN

You're joking, of course?

RALPH

Not a bit. I refereed an interesting paper recently
about modelling grief. I'll email you a copy.

HELEN

Ah, I'm having a bit of trouble with my email at the
moment.

RALPH

Aren't you on the university network? You'll need it to communicate with your students.

HELEN

The English Department secretary did say something about it . . .

RALPH

I'll call the IT centre today and tell them to get on your case.

HELEN

Thank you very much.

RALPH

Meanwhile I'll leave you to your book. (*He gets up.*) What is it?

HELEN

Henry James, *The Wings of the Dove.*

RALPH

I think I saw the film.

HELEN

It's not quite the same.

RALPH

I never got on with Henry James. I prefer his brother, William. Have any of your books been filmed?

HELEN

I'm afraid not. One was optioned, but nothing came of it.

RALPH

What was it called?

HELEN

The Eye of the Storm.

RALPH

I must see if Carrie's got it. She reads a lot of novels. I'll print out that bereavement article and send it to you through the internal mail.

HELEN

Thank you.

RALPH *goes.* HELEN *opens her book and begins to read.* RALPH *returns.*

RALPH

Unless you'd like to come with me now and pick it up.

HELEN

Oh.

RALPH

I could give you a quick tour of the Institute.

HELEN

Aren't you busy?

RALPH

Not for the next hour.

HELEN

Well, that's very kind . . . All right. I must admit I am rather curious about that building.

RALPH

The outside is probably more interesting than the inside. Unlike the brain, which it's supposed to represent . . . the divided dome being the brain's two hemispheres.

HELEN

Oh, I wondered about that . . .

They go off.

Scene Six

RALPH'S *office.* RALPH *ushers* HELEN *in.*

RALPH

Here we are. Can I take your coat?

HELEN

Thank you.

He takes her coat and hangs it up, with his own. She keeps her book in her hand.

RALPH
So what d'you think of the Institute?

HELEN
I'm impressed. The design is stunning.

RALPH
Our students call it the Mind–Body Shop.

HELEN
The ones I saw downstairs seem happy to be here.

RALPH
So they should be . . . There's nowhere else like it in this country. Please sit down.

HELEN
But aren't you worried about the future – with the cuts in university funding?

RALPH
That will mainly affect undergraduate courses. We have only postgraduates and post-docs here, many from abroad. The Institute was endowed by a big software company, and we get a lot of research contracts from industry and government, especially the MOD. So no, I'm not worried about the future.

HELEN
Lucky you.

RALPH
I believe we make our own luck. (HELEN *considers whether to challenge this*). Mostly. Now let me find that article . . .

*As the dialogue continues, *RALPH* boots up his PC, searches for a file, and prints it out.*

HELEN
Why is the outside of the building clad in mirror glass?

RALPH
Can't you guess?

HELEN

Because you can see out of it, but not into it? Like the mind?

RALPH

Right! But after dark, when the lights are on, you can see everything that's going on inside the building, symbolising the explanatory power of scientific research. At least, that was the architect's idea.

HELEN

So if you close the blinds, you ruin the symbolism.

RALPH

Not really. Most thought takes place behind blinds. We can never know for certain what another person is really thinking.

HELEN

Never?

RALPH

Even if they tell us, we don't know whether they're telling the truth. And by the same token, nobody can know our thoughts as we know them.

HELEN

Just as well, perhaps.

RALPH

Absolutely. Imagine what the VC's dinner party would have been like, if all the guests had those bubbles over their heads you get in comics, with their thoughts in them.

HELEN

I suppose that's why people read novels – to find out what goes on in other people's minds.

RALPH

But that's not real knowledge.

HELEN

Oh, isn't it?

RALPH

Real knowledge is based on verifiable facts. The
trouble is, if you restrict the study of consciousness
to what can be objectively observed and measured
– whether it's the behaviour of rats in a maze, or
neurons firing in the human brain – then you leave
out what's distinctive about it.

HELEN

Qualia.

RALPH

Exactly. There's an old joke that crops up in nearly
every book on the subject, about two behaviourist
psychologists who have sex, and afterwards one says
to the other, 'It was great for you, how was it for me?'

HELEN *laughs.*

RALPH

Consciousness is a first-person phenomenon. It always
belongs to an 'I'. 'I feel hungry, I feel anxious, I feel
bored . . .' Scientific description is always third-person:
'The bored subject yawned at irregular intervals.'
That's the problem in a nutshell. How can you describe
a first-person phenomenon in a third-person discourse?

HELEN

Oh, but novelists have been doing that for two
hundred years!

RALPH

How?

HELEN

It's called free indirect style. Listen. (*She opens her
copy of* The Wings of the Dove *at the first page, and
reads aloud.*) 'She waited, Kate Croy, for her father to
come, but he kept her unconscionably, and there were
moments at which she showed herself, in the glass over
the mantel, a face positively pale with the irritation that
had brought her to the point of going away without
sight of him. It was at this point, however, that she
remained; changing her place, moving from the shabby

sofa to the armchair upholstered in a glazed cloth
that gave at once – she had tried it – the sense of the
slippery and the sticky.' You see – you have Kate's
consciousness there, her thoughts, her feelings, her
impatience, her hesitation about leaving or staying,
her perception of her own appearance in the mirror,
the nasty texture of the armchair's upholstery, 'at once
slippery and sticky' – how's that for qualia? And yet
it's all narrated in the third person, in precise, elegant,
well-formed sentences. It's subjective *and* objective.

RALPH

It's effectively done, I grant you. But Henry James
can claim to know what's going on in Kate . . .
what's-her-name's head because he put it there. If she
were a real human being, he could never presume to
tell us how she felt about that armchair.

HELEN

Could a cognitive scientist tell us, then?

RALPH

In the present state of the art, no. For the time
being we have to settle for knowing less about
consciousness than novelists pretend to know.

*He collects the pages from the printer, staples them and gives them
to her.*

RALPH

There you are.

HELEN

Thank you. (*reads title*) 'The Cognitive Architecture
of Emotional States with Special Reference to Grief'.

RALPH

It's only a theoretical model of course.

HELEN

They're not actually trying to build a computer that
feels grief?

RALPH

It's what they're working towards.

HELEN
What on earth for?

RALPH
Emotional Intelligence. It's what human beings
have – we don't just think, we feel. Emotions affect
our priorities, and our decision-making. Computers
have pure intelligence. In many ways they're more
intelligent than we are, and they're getting better all
the time, exponentially. Your laptop – my mobile
phone, even – is smarter than this university's first
mainframe computer, which filled a whole room.
It's been calculated that if cars had developed over
the last thirty years at the same rate as computers,
you'd be able to buy a Rolls-Royce today for under
a pound, and it would do three million miles to the
gallon. It's only a matter of time before computers
start designing themselves, and take over the world,
so it's in our interest to ensure that they evolve with
emotional intelligence built in. Otherwise they might
decide to exterminate us.

HELEN (*laughs*)
That's pure science fiction!

RALPH
Well, a lot of science fiction has proved prophetic.

HELEN
So one day we'll have computers that cry as well as
count?

RALPH
That would be difficult. We don't really understand
why humans produce tears when they're sad. Animals
don't. As Darwin said, 'Crying is a puzzler.'

HELEN (*taken with the phrase*)
'Crying is a puzzler.' When did he say that?

RALPH
It's in the notebooks. I was reading it yesterday. (*He
picks up from his desk a book with a bookmark in it,*

opens it and turns back a few pages as he speaks.) He's
thinking about laughter – how, when humans laugh,
they expose their canine teeth, just like baboons.
He speculates that our laughing and smiling might
be traced back to the way apes communicate the
discovery of food to the rest of their tribe. Here
it is. 'This way of viewing the subject important
– laughing modified barking – smiling modified
laughing.' Then comes the afterthought. He can't
think what crying might be a modification of.
'Crying is a puzzler.'

HELEN
'Sunt lacrymae rerum.'

RALPH
My Latin's a tad rusty.

HELEN
'There are tears of things.' Virgil. It's almost
untranslatable, but one knows what he means.
Something like, 'Crying is a puzzler.'

There is an electronic noise from the doorway. RALPH *and* HELEN
*turn towards it. A small robot on wheels whizzes in and stops in
the middle of the room.*

RALPH
Ah! This is Arthur, our latest recruit.

The robot's lens-like head rotates slowly.

HELEN
What's he doing?

RALPH
Learning his way around. He's mapping the room,
committing it to memory.

*The robot suddenly sets off at speed, collides with something and is
motionless.* HELEN *laughs.* RALPH *frowns.*

RALPH
There must be something wrong with the program.

HELEN

I'd say he has a long way to go before he can get
emotionally involved with another robot.

RALPH

Oh, he's a very simple fellow. We shall be pleased if
we can teach him to pick up litter.

An alarm bell rings, lights blink on and off.

HELEN

What's happened?

RALPH

I wish I knew. (*The telephone rings. He picks it up.*)
Messenger . . . Yes, what's the problem? . . . A
mouse? How could a – Oh, you mean a *real* mouse?
With four legs and whiskers? . . . I see . . . Yes, yes,
I'm coming. (*He puts down the phone.*) A mouse
gnawed through a cable in our network centre.

HELEN

Is it serious?

RALPH

For the mouse, yes, he's dead. Electrocuted. And
our main server is down. I'd better go and assess the
damage.

HELEN

Of course. I'll be going. (*She takes her coat.*)

RALPH

If we don't get email back soon my staff will begin to
have withdrawal symptoms. And I won't forget *your*
email problem.

HELEN

Thank you.

Music.

Scene Seven

HELEN's *flat. She is seated at her table, typing on her laptop. She stops typing and speaks as before.*

HELEN

Apparently scientists have decided that consciousness is a 'problem' which has to be 'solved'. This was news to me, and not particularly welcome. Consciousness is what most novels are *about*, certainly mine. Consciousness is my bread and butter. I rather resent the idea of science poking its nose into it.

When I type 'science' I often leave out the first 'e' by mistake, so it reads like 'skince', and I'm tempted to leave it like that. 'Skince' expresses the cold, pitiless, reductive character of scientific explanations of the world. I feel this quality in Ralph Messenger. When he said about Martin's death, 'For him it was a good way to go,' I nearly got up and walked away. But I didn't.

He offered to show me round his Institute, and while I was there he gave me an article about grief, which he seemed to think I would find interesting. I've never read such an alienating piece of prose in my life. (*She picks up the article and reads.*) 'We define grief as an extended process of cognitive reorganisation characterised by the occurrence of negatively valenced perturbant states caused by an attachment structure reacting to a death event.' So now we know. That was what I went through in the months after Martin's death: just a spot of cognitive reorganisation. The desolating loneliness, the helpless weeping, the booby traps of memory triggered at every turn . . . Halfway through the article there was a diagram supposed to represent the architecture of the mind, all boxes and circles and ellipses, connected by a tangle of swirling arrows and dotted lines – meant to show the reaction of an 'attachment structure' to a 'death event'. I suppose 'attachment structure' is the cognitive science term for love.

Crossfade to RALPH. *Overlap sound of tape playback at the beginning of next scene.* HELEN *goes out.*

Scene Eight

Morning. RALPH*'s office. He reclines in his swivel chair with his recorder in his hand, listening to the playback of his first recording.*

> *'Apparently her husband died suddenly about a year ago . . . There she goes, round the corner of Biology. Wonder where she's going, what she's doing, at ten fifteen on a wet Sunday morning, must be lonely as hell living here on her own . . . I could go after her now, pretend to bump into her, or say "I just happened to see you from my office window, we didn't really have much chance to talk yesterday evening . . ." Why not?'*

Click on tape as recording stops. RALPH *begins new recording.*

RALPH
It's Thursday the 24th of February. I came in early this morning and listened to the tape I recorded last Sunday . . . I must say it was absolutely riveting . . . especially the stuff about Isabel Hennessey . . . Dead now, poor Isabel, breast cancer somebody told me, rotten luck . . . She had nice ones too, 'lovely three-dimensional objects', I remember saying, as I eased off her bra . . . I wonder what happened to that tape of us making love . . . I'd like to listen to it again, and masturbate in her memory, poor Isabel Hennessey . . . (*Pause.*) Full stop. Well, death is a full stop . . . Enough of that, enough of that . . . So, yes, it was fascinating, but of doubtful value to cognitive science . . . It's not just that the experiment partly dictates the content of your thoughts – you can never truly record the act of thinking. When you articulate a

25

thought in speech it always lags behind the formation
of the thought itself, which is like an editorial meeting
between different parts of the brain, behind closed
doors . . . Never mind, it's worth persevering with for
a bit, something useful may emerge, perhaps about
the nature of attention. Like when I was distracted by
the sight of Helen Reed wandering forlornly across the
campus in the rain . . . It turns out that she went into
the faith centre . . . she doesn't believe any more but
still hankers after personal immortality, like so many
people, even some scientists, in spite of the death
of God . . . Incidentally, is that perhaps the second
best-known sentence in the history of philosophy,
Nietzsche's 'God is dead'? It ought to be . . . I thought
for a moment she was going to walk away in a huff
when I said her husband's sudden death was a good
way to go – on reflection, it *was* a little tactless – but
I coaxed her back. She's smart, good-looking too,
but there's something repressed and self-denying
about her, I bet she hasn't had sex since he died . . . I
wonder how long *I* would abstain if Carrie were to die
suddenly? I'd be grief-stricken, of course, and perhaps
I would lose all interest in sex for a while, but I doubt
it . . . More likely to seek relief in another woman's
arms, *'Please stay the night, I just want somebody to hold
me* . . .' What a line, irresistible . . . and of course I
would inherit most of Carrie's money, I would be rich,
as well as free to fuck other women without guilt or
fear of discovery . . . Helen Reed, for example . . . If
Carrie could hear me now she would kill me. It's a
good example of the secrecy of consciousness . . . it's
the filing cabinet to which I alone have the key, and
thank Christ for that . . .

*The telephone rings. He switches off the recorder and picks up the
phone.*

RALPH
Messenger.

Scene Nine

HELEN's *flat and* RALPH's *office.* HELEN, *wearing sweatpants and an old jumper, has the contents of a large envelope in one hand and the telephone in the other.*

HELEN

Oh, hello. This is Helen Reed.

RALPH

Ah. I was just thinking about you.

HELEN

Were you? What were you thinking?

RALPH

Er . . . I was wondering if you've been connected to the university network.

HELEN

Well, that's it actually. I've received something called an Induction Pack from the IT centre with a lot of instructions, and frankly I can't make head nor tail of it.

RALPH

I'll come round and sort it out for you.

HELEN

Well, that's very kind. When would be convenient?

RALPH

I'll come now.

HELEN

Now?

RALPH

I'm free now.

HELEN

Well, thank you. But I feel I'm imposing on you.

RALPH

Not at all. I know the block. What number are you?

HELEN

Seven.

27

Act One Scene Nine

RALPH

I'll be over in about fifteen minutes.

HELEN

Right.

Both replace telephone receivers. HELEN, *conscious of her unflattering clothes, goes into her bedroom.* RALPH *puts his recorder in a drawer of his desk and locks it, takes his coat, and leaves the office.*

Music.

Scene Ten

HELEN's *flat. Doorbell chimes. Sounds of their greetings, off.* HELEN, *in changed clothes, ushers* RALPH, *into the room. He looks round.*

RALPH

It's the first time I've been inside one of these flats. It's quite cosy, isn't it?

HELEN

I wouldn't call it 'cosy', exactly. It's convenient.

RALPH

Won't you show me round? As a member of Senate I ought to know what kind of accommodation we offer our visiting faculty.

HELEN

There's nothing much to show. My bedroom is in here.

RALPH (*peers in*)

Immaculate! If I were living here on my own it would be a complete tip within a week.

HELEN

Kitchen and bathroom off the hall. (*points*)

RALPH

And this is where you write.

He goes over to the table with the laptop, which is open and switched on. Beside it are the envelope and papers HELEN *was holding in the previous scene.*

HELEN
Yes.

RALPH
May I?

HELEN
Please.

RALPH *(sits down, picks up the papers)*
These are the instructions they sent you?

HELEN
Yes. It's very kind of you to help me out. I'm afraid
I'm hopeless with computers. Martin used to do all
this sort of thing for me.

As the dialogue continues, RALPH *installs the email software. He
makes rapid keystrokes, pauses to wait for the next prompt, then
more rapid keystrokes, and so on, occasionally using the mouse
and glancing at the instructions.*

RALPH
Are you working on a new novel?

HELEN
No. Since Martin died . . . I did start one, but it
didn't work. Making up fictitious characters and
inventing things for them to do seems so futile after
something like that happens.

RALPH
You've got to get over it, you know.

HELEN
Yes, everybody tells me that.

RALPH
So what are you writing?

HELEN
A kind of journal. Just to keep the writing muscles
exercised.

RALPH
Your secret thoughts, eh?

HELEN

Well, it's not for publication.

RALPH (*consults instructions*)

Your user name is 'reed h t'. (*types it in*) Remember that.

HELEN

Right. 'Reed h t'.

RALPH

No dots or spaces. (*continues typing*) What does the 't' stand for?

HELEN

Teresa. My mother is devoted to the Little Flower.

RALPH

What flower is that?

HELEN

Saint Teresa of Lisieux. She's called the Little Flower.

RALPH

Oh. (*types*) So your address will be: 'h dot t dot reed at Harro dot ac dot uk.'

HELEN

And I can use that for email anywhere? Not just within the university?

RALPH

Absolutely.

HELEN

That's wonderful. I'm fed up with my email provider.

RALPH

They've given you a password, but you'd better change it.

HELEN

Why?

RALPH

Because I've seen it, so I could hack into your email. (*He gets up and yields the seat to her.*) Not that I would, of course. Just type it into the box there. It has to have between eight and twelve characters.

HELEN *sits down, stares at the screen and thinks.*

HELEN

Ummm . . .

RALPH

Though I would be tempted.

HELEN

What?

RALPH

To read your emails. (HELEN *is surprised.*) It might be grist to my mill. Data for consciousness studies.

HELEN

I don't see how.

RALPH

Well, you might, for instance, write to your friends describing your feelings about being here much more openly than you would to me. Or perhaps the opposite, pretending to be happier than you are. Of course your journal would be even more revealing, but email would be better than nothing.

HELEN

Then I shall guard my password very carefully. (*She types in her password with deliberation.*) Shall I click on 'Continue' now?

RALPH

Yes. I'll just finish it off.

HELEN *gets up and* RALPH *sits down in her place. She stands behind him and looks at the screen as he types rapidly.*

RALPH

As soon as you boot up you'll be connected to the university network. (*moves mouse*) Click on this icon for email, and this one for the Internet.

HELEN

Thank you so much. Can I offer you a cup of coffee?

RALPH (*glances at watch*)

Thanks, but I've got a supervision at ten thirty. What are you doing next Sunday?

HELEN

Well . . . nothing.

RALPH

We have a cottage in the country we go to most Sundays. Would you like to join us?

HELEN

That would be very nice, but . . .

RALPH:

What?

HELEN

Shouldn't you check with your wife?

RALPH

It was Carrie's idea. She enjoyed talking to you at the VC's dinner.

HELEN

Then I'll be glad to come.

RALPH

Good. We'll pick you up at about ten.

HELEN

Thank you.

RALPH

Bring a swimming costume.

HELEN

You have a pool?

> RALPH
> A hot tub.

> HELEN
> Ah.

> RALPH
> Till Sunday, then.

> HELEN
> I look forward to it.

RALPH goes out, escorted by HELEN. They exchange goodbyes off. Sound of front door shutting. After a pause HELEN returns carrying a faded, much-used swimming costume, and holds it out for inspection. She goes into the bedroom.

Scene Eleven

The campus. RALPH takes out his mobile. He keys in a memorised number.

> RALPH
> Carrie? Look, I just ran into that writer, Helen what's-her-name, you met her at the VC's dinner . . . Helen Reed, that's right. She's having problems with email, so I offered to help her . . . She seems a bit lonely. I thought we might invite her out to the cottage next Sunday . . . yeah . . . OK, I'll see to it . . . Yes, I'll tell her to bring a costume . . . No, I won't forget . . . OK, see you.

He ends the call, pockets the phone and goes off smiling to himself.

Music.

Scene Twelve

The deck of the Messengers' country cottage. RALPH in swimming trunks, and HELEN, in a new swimming costume, recline facing each other in a hot tub. Snow is falling.

HELEN (*looking up*)
This is blissful! Lolling in a hot bath while watching
snowflakes falling through the sky. And the bathwater
never gets cold!

RALPH
It has a thermostat . . . I read an article once, in a
cognitive science journal, called 'What is it like to
be a thermostat?' (HELEN *laughs*.) This guy argued
that anything that processes information, in however
humble a way, could be described as conscious.

CARRIE'S VOICE (*off*)
Messenger! Lunch in fifteen minutes.

RALPH (*calls*)
OK!

HELEN
I should go and help.

RALPH
No, stay here. Carrie doesn't like other people in her
kitchen when she's serving up a meal.

HELEN
So do you think this tub is conscious?

RALPH
Not self-conscious. Unlike us, it doesn't know it's
having a good time.

HELEN
I thought there was no such thing as the self.

RALPH
No such 'thing', no. There's no ghost in the machine.

HELEN
That's such a loaded phrase. I don't believe in ghosts,
but I believe in selves.

RALPH
Of course there are selves – we invent them all the
time. It's something we humans do with our spare
brain capacity.

HELEN

What d'you mean, 'spare'?

RALPH

The cognitive power of the human brain is much,
much greater than that of any other animal on the
planet, for reasons we don't yet understand – it's
not just a matter of size. This gave our primitive
ancestors a huge evolutionary advantage over
other species. Men gradually dominated the rest of
Nature. They learned to make tools and weapons, to
communicate through language, to solve problems
by running various options through their mental
software, instead of just reacting instinctively. They
got beyond the four Fs.

HELEN

The four Fs?

RALPH

Fighting, fleeing, feeding and . . . mating.

HELEN

Oh. (*She laughs.*)

RALPH

But primitive man was like a guy who's been given a
state-of-the-art computer and just uses it to do simple
arithmetic. Sooner or later he's going to discover he
can do all kinds of other things as well. That's what
we did with our brains, in due course. We developed
trade, and laws, and culture. But before that, we
became aware of ourselves as individuals, with a past
and a future. We became *self*-conscious. And there's
a downside to that: we know we're going to die.
Imagine what a terrible shock it was to Neanderthal
man, or Cro-Magnon man, or whoever it was that
first clocked the dreadful truth: that one day he
would be meat. Lions and tigers don't know that.
Apes don't know it. We do.

HELEN

Elephants must know. They have graveyards.

RALPH

I'm afraid that's a myth. *Homo sapiens* was the first and only living being to discover he was mortal. So how does he respond? He makes up stories to explain how he got into this fix, and how he might get out of it. He invents religion, he develops burial customs, he makes up stories about the afterlife, and the immortality of the soul. As time goes on, these stories get more and more elaborate. But in the most recent phase of culture, seconds ago in terms of evolutionary history, science suddenly takes off, and starts to tell a different story about how we got here, a much more powerful story that knocks the religious one for six. Really intelligent people don't believe the religious story any more, but they still cling to some of its consoling concepts, like the soul, life after death, and so on.

HELEN

I think that's what really irks you, isn't it? That most people go on stubbornly believing that there *is* a ghost in the machine, a self or soul, however many times scientists and philosophers tell them there isn't.

RALPH

It doesn't 'irk' me, exactly.

HELEN

Oh yes it does. It's as if you're determined to eradicate the idea from the face of the earth. Like an Inquisitor trying to root out heresy.

RALPH

I just think we shouldn't confuse what we would like to be the case with what *is* the case.

HELEN

But you admit that we have thoughts that are private, secret, known only to ourselves.

RALPH

Oh yes.

HELEN

You admit that my experience of this moment, lolling
here in hot water, under the open sky as the snow
falls, is not exactly the same as yours?

RALPH

I can see where this argument is going. You're saying,
there's something it is like to be you, or to be me,
some quality of experience that is unique to you or to
me, that can't be described objectively or explained
in purely physical terms. So one might as well call it
an immaterial self or soul.

HELEN

I suppose so, yes. But –

RALPH

And I'm saying it's still a machine. A virtual machine
in a biological machine.

HELEN

So everything's a machine?

RALPH

Everything that processes information, yes.

HELEN

I think that's a horrifying idea.

RALPH (*smiles*)

You're a machine that's been programmed by culture
not to recognise that it's a machine.

CARRIE'S VOICE (*off*)

Messenger!

LITTLE GIRL'S VOICE (*off*)

Come *on*, Daddy!

HELEN

We'd better get out.

RALPH

Hang on. I'll get you a robe.

*He gets out of the tub, puts on a towelling robe and holds one out
for* HELEN. *She steps out and shrugs it on.*

Act One Scene Twelve

HELEN

Thank you.

RALPH

Helen . . .

As she turns to face him he embraces her and kisses her on the lips. She does not resist.

Blackout. Music.

Scene Thirteen

Late afternoon. HELEN*'s flat and* RALPH*'s office.* RALPH *reclines in his swivel chair, reading a book.* HELEN *is sitting at the table, with a pile of folders beside her laptop. She types, then stops and speaks as before.*

HELEN

I've spent all day yesterday and most of today reading
the students' novels-in-progress, and I feel rather
jaded by the experience. It's a very unnatural way to
read, of course, jumping from one unfinished story
to another, but it made me think about the prolific
production of fiction in our culture. Are we in danger
of accumulating a fiction mountain – an immense
quantity of surplus novels, like the butter mountains
and wine lakes of the EU? It's frightening to think
of how many novels I must have read in my lifetime,
and how little I retain of the substance of most of
them. Should I really be encouraging these bright
young people to add their quotient to the dustheap
of forgotten fiction? Will my own work end up there?
(*She resumes typing.*)

RALPH *closes his book and picks up the recorder.*

RALPH

March the third. It's four thirty in the afternoon and
I'm killing time before I have to attend an inaugural
lecture by the new professor of metallurgy. I've

been reading Hoberman's latest book on the brain.
It's not as good as his first one, but why should he
worry? He won the Nobel Prize in Physiology three
years ago . . . Hard to imagine anyone in AI getting
a Nobel. Even if somebody cracked the problem of
consciousness tomorrow, which prize would they give
him? Physics? Chemistry? Physiology? It doesn't fit
any of the categories . . . Or rather, it embraces them
all – all science takes place within consciousness.
That's why it's so fascinating . . . I wonder what
it's like to win a Nobel . . . the quale of Nobelness.
Well, I'll never know . . . not even an FRS in realistic
prospect . . .

HELEN
I must admit I've found it hard to concentrate on the
students' work because I keep thinking all the time
about THAT KISS, last Sunday. I was taken totally
by surprise – we'd been having such an intellectual
argument . . . I felt his foot touch mine once or twice
in the hot tub, but I thought it was just accidental,
it never crossed my mind that he had any amorous
intentions. Perhaps he finds it sexually stimulating,
a woman standing up to him in debate. The kiss
was firmly mouth on mouth – not passionate, not
intrusive, but definitely sexual. And I accepted it. At
least, I didn't resist it. I didn't slap his face or push
him away, or ask him what he thought he was doing.
I didn't say a word. Perhaps I even responded a little
. . . Perhaps? A little? My whole body seemed to melt
inside. Of course, my life has been rather sparsely
furnished with kisses lately . . .

RALPH
I know what they say about me behind my back:
'*a populariser, a media don, some flashy books to his
name but no serious original research . . .*' Some truth
in that. Perhaps I love the life of the body too much
. . . Your true scientist thinks only of his science . . .
I also think about women, food, wine . . . especially

women . . . I kissed her, Helen . . . after the others
had gone back into the house, we stayed in the tub
chatting, or rather arguing . . . that's what I like about
her, she's prepared to argue about serious subjects
. . . until eventually Carrie called us in for lunch,
and as I was helping her on with a robe I kissed her
. . . I took a chance, but my instinct is usually right
with these things . . . She seemed to enjoy it . . . She
looked good in her swimming costume . . . They're
funny garments, though – how little they cover, and
yet what a difference they make. It's always a surprise
when you see a woman completely naked for the first
time . . . I'd very much like to see Helen Reed naked.
I don't think I'd be disappointed.

*He switches off the recorder, pulls his chair up to the desk and
checks his email on the PC.*

HELEN

Carrie didn't see us kiss, and needless to say I
didn't tell her. So it's there, now, a secret between
us, something Ralph knows and I know, but Carrie
doesn't. When he handed me the mint sauce at lunch
and our eyes met, the knowledge passed between
us silently and invisibly – not just that we'd kissed,
but also that we had tacitly agreed to conceal it. We
didn't betray to the others what had happened by so
much as the flicker of an eyelid or slightest tremor of
the voice. How adept at deception we human beings
are, how easily it comes to us. Did it come with self-
consciousness? Was that the real Fall of Man? There's
something horribly plausible about his arguments
– I hate them but I find it hard to refute them.
For instance, religion arising out of man's unique
awareness of his own mortality. I googled elephant
graveyards, and he's right, dammit, they're a myth.
But I have absolutely no intention of embarking on
an affair with Ralph Messenger, let's be quite clear
about that. For one thing, I like Carrie a lot. And
they have a lovely family, two boys and a sweet little

girl. They all call him 'Messenger'. I was invited to come again next Sunday.

RALPH *dials a number on his desk telephone. The phone on* HELEN*'s desk rings. She picks it up.*

HELEN

Hello?

RALPH

It's Messenger.

HELEN

Oh, hello.

RALPH

Have you checked your email lately?

HELEN

Not today.

RALPH

Not for a whole day? Doesn't your laptop ping when you have incoming email?

HELEN

I keep it muted when I'm working. Did you send me an email, then?

RALPH

Two.

HELEN

Oh, I'm sorry. What did they say?

RALPH

They said, is your email working all right?

HELEN

Well, it is, thanks.

RALPH

What about the Internet?

HELEN

Well, that is a bit of a problem. I get a message saying 'Windows cannot open this page'.

RALPH

That's not right. Why didn't you tell me before?

HELEN

I didn't like to bother you.

RALPH

I'll come round and investigate.

HELEN

Well, that's very kind. Are you sure you can spare the time?

RALPH

I'll come tomorrow in my lunch hour.

HELEN

I wouldn't want you to miss your lunch.

RALPH

You could give me lunch. Have you got a bit of bread and cheese in the house?

HELEN

Well, yes, but –

RALPH

That will do perfectly. I'll be round at about twelve forty-five.

HELEN

All right.

RALPH

See you then. I'll bring some wine.

RALPH *puts down the phone, pleased with himself, and goes out.*

HELEN *puts down the phone, a little flustered but pleased, and goes into the kitchen.*

Music.

Scene Fourteen

HELEN's *flat.* HELEN *and* RALPH *come in from the direction of the kitchen, with glasses half full of red wine in their hands.* RALPH *also holds the open bottle, two-thirds empty.*

> RALPH
>
> That was a delicious lunch. I asked for simple bread and cheese, and I got soup and salad and a veritable cheeseboard.

> HELEN
>
> You were lucky. I needed to go food shopping this morning anyway. Thank you for sorting out the Internet connection.

> RALPH
>
> My pleasure. (*He glances at the laptop.*) Still writing your journal?

> HELEN
>
> Yes.

> RALPH
>
> I suppose you're making notes on all of us?

> HELEN
>
> No.

> RALPH
>
> Really? You mean there's nothing about me in there?

> HELEN
>
> Well, inevitably there are . . . references to people I've met, like you and Carrie.

> RALPH
>
> Good. I should feel quite humiliated otherwise.
> (*Pause.*) I started keeping a kind of journal, recently.

> HELEN
>
> Did you?

> RALPH
>
> It began as a bit of consciousness research. The idea was to generate some raw data. I just dictated my thoughts into a tape recorder as they occurred to me.

HELEN

'Let us record the atoms as they fall upon the mind in the order in which they fall.'

RALPH

Who said that?

HELEN

Virginia Woolf.

RALPH

I bet she didn't, though. I bet she jiggled the order about to suit herself. And rendered it all in beautiful, much-polished prose.

HELEN

Yes, she probably did. But she was trying to produce the illusion of a stream of consciousness –

RALPH

I wasn't trying to produce an illusion, I was after the real thing. It's difficult though – impossible really. The brain does a lot of ordering and editing before the first words come out of your mouth.

HELEN

So you abandoned the experiment?

RALPH

No, I still dictate something every now and again. It's become a habit.

HELEN

Are you making notes on me?

RALPH (*without hesitation*)

Yes.

HELEN

Then we're even. Would you like some coffee?

RALPH

Maybe in a minute. Let's enjoy the last of the wine. Will you have some more?

HELEN

No thanks. I'm not going to be fit for anything this afternoon, as it is. I shall probably fall asleep.

RALPH

What a good idea. I wouldn't mind a siesta myself.

HELEN

Haven't you got work to do this afternoon?

RALPH

All I've got is a boring committee meeting which I should be very glad to skip.

Pause.

HELEN

I don't want to have an affair with you, Ralph.

RALPH

Why not?

HELEN

I don't approve of adultery.

RALPH

Well, as long as it's not because you don't find me attractive . . . I find *you* very attractive, Helen. In fact I think I'm falling in love with you.

HELEN

You must fall in love very easily.

RALPH

Well, I do. And I flatter myself that I'm a good lover.

HELEN

I don't think we should go on with this conversation.

RALPH

We could go into your bedroom and take off our clothes and lie down on the bed and make love very slowly and enjoyably, and fall asleep in each other's arms, and wake refreshed and renewed. Nobody else would ever know about it.

HELEN

No. I won't.

RALPH

You know we're attracted to each other. It happened
the first evening we met, at the VC's dinner party,
don't deny it.

HELEN

We can't just do what we want without regard to
other people.

RALPH

If you mean Carrie . . .

HELEN

Yes, I do. I wouldn't want to deceive her.

RALPH

We deceive each other all the time, Helen. There
are a hundred things you wouldn't tell Carrie in any
circumstances. Why make a fetish of this one?

HELEN

That's the way I am. It's probably my Catholic
upbringing.

RALPH

But you don't believe all that nonsense any more.
You don't believe you'll go to hell just because one
afternoon, after a very pleasant meal, you went into
your bedroom with me and very pleasantly fucked.
Do you?

HELEN

No, but . . .

RALPH

It's the supremely human act, freely to fuck, not
because you're on heat, or in oestrus, like an animal,
but to give and receive pleasure with someone you like.

HELEN

I'll make coffee and then you'd better go to your
committee meeting.

RALPH (*glances at wristwatch*)
If I'm going to the committee meeting I'll have to
skip the coffee.

HELEN
All right.

RALPH
You're sure you wouldn't prefer me to skip the
committee?

HELEN
Quite sure.

RALPH
Well, I'm sorry. I think it would have been . . .
memorable. See you on Sunday, then?

HELEN
I don't think I can come this weekend.

RALPH
But you're expected!

HELEN
I'll see.

RALPH
I'll let myself out. Thanks for the lunch. (*He goes
towards the front door, stops and turns.*) Do come on
Sunday. (*He goes out.*)

HELEN *is pensive. She sits at her desk and opens her laptop. She
types and then speaks, as before.*

HELEN
Ralph Messenger left just now, after trying and
failing to get me to go to bed with him. It was a
close call – closer, I suspect, than he realised. He's
the first man I've met since Martin died who I can
imagine myself naked with, making love, without
the image seeming absurd or repellent . . . He didn't
attempt to kiss me again, though I was half hoping he
would. He behaved like a perfect gentleman. Except
that after lunch he coolly proposed that we should go

into my bedroom and, as he put it, 'very pleasantly fuck'. Oh dear, just repeating those words makes me melt inside again.

Is he right? Have I pointlessly denied myself an experience from which I might have risen, as he said, 'refreshed and renewed'? God knows I could do with some refreshment and renewal – my body craves to be held and stroked and comforted.

Sometimes I think I'm struggling with Ralph Messenger for my soul – literally, because according to him, it doesn't exist. Not in the sense of an immortal, essential self, answerable to its creator for its actions. So why be good? Why deny oneself pleasure? One of the Karamazovs says, '*If there is no God, everything is permitted.*' Is that true? Then why don't we rob, rape and cheat each other all the time? Enlightened self-interest, the atheists say – because we increase our personal chances of survival by accepting social constraints. But not in sex, not any more, they say. There's no need to pretend that sex for pleasure should be confined to monogamous marriage. True? Not if contemporary fiction is to be believed. There seems to be just as much anger, jealousy and bitterness caused by infidelity as there ever was.

If I could be a hundred per cent sure that Carrie would never find out, and therefore never be hurt, perhaps I would sleep with Ralph, but there is no such thing as certainty in human relations. Unfortunately. (*She continues to type.*)

Fade to black.

ACT TWO

Scene One

RALPH's *office and* HELEN's *flat. They are both seated at their desks, using their computers, exchanging emails, which are projected onto a screen or screens as they type, with amplified sound of the keystrokes. When the message is complete, the writer presses the 'Send' key and the message disappears. The other writer then composes a reply and sends it in the same way. The usual automatic email headings appear above the first two messages – only the word 'cold' in* RALPH's *first email heading needs to be typed in by him.* RALPH's *messages have uncorrected typos.*

> From: Ralph Messenger
> To: Helen Reed
> Subject: cold
> Date: 10 March 9:08:31
>
> Hi helen, we missed you at the cottage yesterday. i hope you're getting over that cold. it must have come on quitesuddenly – you looked fine on friday. many thanks for the lunch.
> best wishes, Ralph
>
> From: Helen Reed
> To: Ralph Messenger
> Subject: cold
> Date:10 March 10:31:13
>
> Dear Ralph,
> My cold is improving, thanks. Regards to Carrie.
> Best wishes,
> Helen
>
> Helen, since your feeling better, what about lunch tomorrow? staff house at 12.45? or a pub if you prefer. ralph
>
> Dear Ralph,
> I think it would be best if we don't meet for a while. You have

made your feelings very plain. I won't pretend that I find them
repugnant, but I can't reciprocate.
Best wishes
Helen

helen, that's ridiculous. i admire your mind as well as your
body. i like kicking ideas around with you. ralph

Can't we kick them around by email?
Helen

ok i was going to put a proposal to you over lunch but here it
is. suppose we swap journals? i show you mine and you show
me yours – complete, uncensored, unedited. what do you say?
ralph

What an extraordinary idea. I wouldn't dream of it. My journal is
not intended for anyone's eyes but mine.
Helen

helen, it seems to me that theres an opportunity here. We've
both been keeping journals since we first met. If we swap we
would each get a unique insight into another person's
consciousness. We could compare our responses to the same
events. I could literally 'read your mind' and you mine.
ralph

Dear Ralph,
I can see what's in it for you. What's in it for me?
Helen.

Helen, surely a novelist, especially a woman novelist, should
jump at the chance to look inside a man's head, to see what
really goes on in there. It's not pretty. It's possible when you've
read my journal you'll nver want to speak to me again, but i hope
not. i believe that like me you value the truth above all else.
ralph

Dear Ralph,
To surrender the privacy of one's mind would be terribly
dangerous. We all have bad, ignoble, shameful thoughts. The
fact that we can keep them to ourselves is essential to
civilisation.
Helen

hey i'm not trying destroy civilisation, Helen, i'm just offering
you a deal, your thoughts for mine, to further our respective
researches into human nature.
Ralph

Dear Ralph,
I'm sorry, but there seems to me something distinctly Faustian
about your compact. I smell a whiff of brimstone about it. The
answer is no.
Best wishes,
Helen

well it was worth a try.
Ralph

Scene Two

RALPH's *office and* HELEN's *flat.* HELEN *is sitting at her desk,
but her laptop is closed.* RALPH *drops an Alka-Seltzer tablet into
a glass of water, drinks, and speaks into his recorder.*

RALPH

It's April the third. I haven't recorded anything for a
while, partly because – (*He belches.*) Pardon! – partly
because I've been too busy planning the conference
we're hosting at the end of the semester, and partly
because nothing interesting has developed in
relation to Helen . . . It's a stand-off . . . I know she
fancies me, but her moral scruples prevent her from
doing anything about it . . . Very frustrating . . .
because I still see a good deal of her, and I like what
I see, especially in a swimming costume . . . She's
become a kind of adopted member of the family,
comes to the cottage nearly every Sunday, but she
sticks to Carrie all the time, or the kids, makes sure
she's never alone with me, especially in the hot tub
. . . She and Carrie go around a lot together . . .
shopping in Harrogate, antique auctions . . . today
they've gone to the Turkish baths. What do they talk
about? Me, I expect, and her dead husband, what's-
his-name, Martin . . . I wonder what they say to

each other . . . My best chance of getting anywhere with her will be in the Easter school holiday, when Carrie and the kids are in California visiting her parents . . . but I need some excuse to see Helen on her own . . . some way of getting under her guard . . . Offering to swap our journals was a bad idea, it frightened her off . . . (*He draws a cartoon thought-bubble in the air above his head with a finger.*) Thinks! The conference . . . I could ask her to do the Last Word . . .

He switches off the recorder and dials a number on his desk telephone. It rings in HELEN*'s flat. She picks up the receiver.*

HELEN

Hello.

RALPH

Helen, it's Messenger. How did you and Carrie get on in the Turkish baths?

HELEN (*slight hesitation*)

Er, fine. It was . . . a revelation.

RALPH

It's a wonderful place, isn't it? They got four stars from . . . whoever it is that gives stars to spas. Look, I have a favour to ask of you. I want you to do something at the ICSA conference.

HELEN

What's the ICSA?

RALPH

The International Cognitive Science Association. We're hosting their annual conference this year, at the end of the semester.

HELEN

What on earth could I possibly contribute to that?

RALPH

Well, that's what I want to explain – but not over the phone. Could we have lunch sometime?

HELEN (*pauses for thought*)
All right.

RALPH
Staff House on Friday?

HELEN
Last time you suggested a pub –

RALPH (*eagerly*)
Would you prefer that?

HELEN
Well, the food at Staff House is not exactly –

RALPH
Absolutely! I know a great little country pub, not far
from here . . . I'll pick you up at about twelve.

HELEN
Right.

RALPH
See you then. (*He puts down the phone, puzzled, but
pleased.*)

Music.

Scene Three

A pub garden. A sunny spring day. RALPH *and* HELEN *are seated at
a table, having finished their lunch. Soiled plates, a bottle of wine
two-thirds empty and glasses are on the table.*

HELEN
'The Last Word'?

RALPH
Yes, that's what it's called in the programme.
Every year we invite somebody to the conference
who's not in the cognitive science racket, but who
we think might have something interesting to say
about consciousness. They listen to all the papers,
then at the end of the conference they give us their

impressions, and their own point of view. We've had a psychiatrist, a quantum physicist, last year we had a Buddhist monk . . . We've never had a novelist. It would be a feather in my cap if you would do it.

HELEN

I couldn't . . .

RALPH

Sure you could.

HELEN

Stand up in front of all those scientists? They'd tear me to pieces.

RALPH

No they won't. They'll be charmed. Anyway, you don't have to answer questions.

HELEN

There's no discussion?

RALPH

No. That's why it's called the Last Word.

HELEN

Well, that does make it less intimidating . . .

RALPH

And it can be as short as you like. Come on, Helen, do this for me. Think of all the hot tubs you've had at the cottage. It's payback time.

HELEN (*considers*)

Well . . . all right.

RALPH

Wonderful. Let's drink to it. (*He empties the bottle into their glasses and they drink.*) I read one of your books yesterday.

HELEN

Did you?

RALPH

I thought it was time. I'll have to introduce you at the conference.

HELEN
Which one did you read?

RALPH
The Eye of the Storm.

HELEN
And what did you think of it?

RALPH
To be honest it's not my kind of thing. It's what I would call a 'woman's book' – though you're not allowed to say that any more. But I could appreciate the skill that went into it.

HELEN (*with a little bow of the head*)
Thank you, kind sir, she said.

RALPH
No, I mean it. You write beautiful sentences. How d'you do it?

HELEN
I read them aloud.

RALPH
Really?

HELEN
Yes. I always tell my students: read your work aloud to yourself before you hand it in. You will *hear* what's wrong with it, what needs revising.

RALPH
But there was one scene when I forgot I was reading sentences, when I was really gripped. Towards the end, when the couple are in Paris.

HELEN (*laughs, a little self-consciously*)
You mean the bedroom scene, with the masks, and the tying up?

RALPH
Yes.

HELEN

I'm afraid that's most people's favourite chapter.
Apart from my parents.

RALPH

Is it autobiographical?

HELEN

Oh, Messenger, you disappoint me. Everybody asks
me that.

RALPH

Well, is it?

HELEN

Martin and I did have a weekend break in Paris once,
in a luxury hotel. And in the chest of drawers in the
bedroom I found two masks and a coil of silken cord,
left behind by the previous occupants. I imagined
what they might have done with them . . .

RALPH

And did you and Martin do anything with them?

HELEN

No. (*He looks at her sceptically.*) If we did, I wouldn't
tell you. (*She turns her face up to the sky.*) What a
wonderful day! The first real day of spring.

RALPH

Far too nice to go back to work.

HELEN

Yes.

Pause.

RALPH

Are you in a hurry to get back?

HELEN

No, I have a free afternoon.

RALPH

So do I.

Pause.

56

We're not far from the cottage here. We could go
there and have a hot tub.

HELEN
I haven't got a swimming costume with me.

RALPH
It's nicer without one, actually.

HELEN
Yes, I expect it is.

RALPH *stares. She meets his gaze frankly.*

RALPH
I'll pay the bill. (*He gets up and goes off quickly.*)

HELEN *remains sitting, and raises her face to the sun, closing her
eyes, a faint smile on her lips.*
Music.

Scene Four

Evening. RALPH *'s office. He is sitting in his swivel chair,
speaking into the recorder.*

RALPH
April the fifth. A day to remember. This afternoon I
fucked one of England's finest contemporary novelists.
That's how she's described on the back of *The Eye
of the Storm.* (*He picks up a paperback and reads from
the back cover.*) '*A novel of exquisite sensibility and
artful restraint, by one of England's finest contemporary
novelists.' The Spectator* . . . Well, she wasn't at all
restrained this afternoon, and I have a love bite on
my left shoulder to prove it. She damn nearly drew
blood . . . I'm going to have to conceal it from Carrie
until she leaves for California on Monday, and hope to
hell the marks fade before she gets back . . . The first
hint I had that I was going to get lucky was when she
called me 'Messenger' in an easy, familiar way – she'd

never done that before. When she agreed to go to the
cottage after lunch and skinny-dip in the hot tub, I
thought to myself that can only mean one thing . . .
It's not easy to drive with an erection, you have to lean
forward over the wheel with your chin practically on
the dashboard . . . As soon as we got inside the cottage
I kissed her and said, 'Let's make love.' 'I've forgotten
how to do it,' she said. 'I'll remind you,' I said, and led
her to the bedroom. I didn't have the faintest idea why
she'd changed her mind, but I didn't want to give her
any time for second thoughts. The sex was passionate
but brief, perhaps because she hadn't had any for a
long time. She came with astonishing rapidity, like
a flash flood, almost as soon as I entered her, and
I didn't hold myself back. I fell asleep immediately
afterwards. When I woke, I found she had covered us
with a sheet. She was lying on her back, with her head
on the pillow, and her face had the soft, blurred look
of a satisfied woman. She gave me a strange little
smile, both shy and wry. 'So, how was it for me?' she
said . . .

Later, when we were naked together in the hot tub,
I wanted to have her again, in the bubbling water,
under the open sky, but she wouldn't. I offered to
take her into the house and tie her up. That's when
she bit me.

Music.

Scene Five

HELEN*'s flat. She is typing on her laptop. She stops, and speaks
as before.*

HELEN
It's some time since I made an entry in this journal.
A journal is a kind of mirror in which you look at
yourself every day, candidly, unflinchingly, and
tell yourself the truth. I haven't felt like doing that
since Messenger and I became lovers. I was afraid it

might awaken scruples of conscience and inhibit my pleasure. So I tried describing what had happened in the third person, free indirect style, as if I were a character in a novel.

She makes some keystrokes on the laptop and the printer extrudes a printed sheet. She takes it and reads it aloud, perhaps like an author giving a public reading.

'For that was what she had become, a woman of pleasure, a woman of easy virtue, a woman no better than she should be – or so she would have been described in the pages of an old novel. Not in a modern one, of course. She was only doing what everybody else was doing, evidently: fulfilling her desires, making hay while the sun shone, squeezing every drop of joy from her body before it was too late, because, as they said, *"This is the only life you will have."* And she couldn't regret it, it had been so exciting. Nerve-racking, too, at times. Carrie's absence had made it possible, but there was always the risk that someone would notice Messenger visiting her block of flats with surprising frequency, or see them out together in some compromising situation. One day he took her to a Stone Age burial site on the top of a hill, and nothing would satisfy him but to spread his cagoule on the side of the barrow and copulate with her like a Stone Age man taking his mate, short and sharp. She had scarcely pulled up her knickers and brushed down her skirt when a party of ramblers with maps and walking sticks came by, smiling and saying "Good afternoon".

'For herself, she much preferred to make love indoors, on a bed, behind drawn curtains, and to sleep afterwards, sated and exhausted. He was surprisingly strong in the arms and shoulders, and flipped her this way and that, over him and under him, like a wrestler practising 'holds'. Sometimes it seemed to her that he wanted to reduce her to a helpless quivering bundle of sensation, until she could bear no more, slapping the mattress like a beaten wrestler.'

Hmm. Rather warm. I never wrote anything like that before.

She puts down the sheet and resumes typing on the laptop for a while, then stops.

Am I falling in love with this man or is it merely lust? It was lust when I agreed to go back to the cottage with him that day. I was still reeling from Carrie's revelation, in the cooling room at the Turkish baths, that she is having an affair herself. She didn't tell me who with, and I didn't want to know. I think she was trying to encourage me to get over my celibate mourning for Martin – not guessing that the only man in the world I want to go to bed with is her husband. Who the very next day offered me a second chance to do so. I didn't hesitate. If Carrie was deceiving Ralph, why shouldn't I deceive Carrie? Just once, I thought to myself, just this once. Only to find myself swept off my feet by the force of a man's passion. We haven't done anything these past two weeks except look for opportunities to make love – he's coming today in his lunch hour. But tomorrow Carrie is coming home from her trip to California, and I have to ask myself: what future is there in this adventure?

The doorbell chimes. She quickly switches off her laptop, waits to see that it shuts down, and closes it. The doorbell chimes again as she goes out to answer the door.

Coming!

Scene Six

HELEN's *flat.* RALPH *comes out of the bedroom, doing up the buttons of his shirt and tucking it in, followed by* HELEN, *in dressing gown, carrying his jacket.*

HELEN (*hands him his jacket*)
Will you be late for your Senate meeting?

RALPH
It doesn't matter. I'm sorry, Helen.

HELEN (*smiles*)
It's all right.

RALPH
I don't know why it happened . . .

HELEN
Don't worry about it. (*lightly*) Perhaps we've
been overdoing it –

RALPH
Nonsense.

HELEN
Or perhaps . . .

RALPH
What?

HELEN
Nothing.

RALPH
What? (HELEN *is silent*.) You think it's because Carrie
is coming back, don't you?

HELEN
Perhaps.

RALPH
Well, it's not.

HELEN
But it's going to make a difference.

RALPH
It will be harder to meet, but we'll find ways.

HELEN
Oh, Messenger, I feel afraid.

RALPH
Don't. (*He embraces her.*) It's probably indigestion.

HELEN (*half laughing, half crying*)
What is?

RALPH
What happened just now. (*He jerks his head towards the bedroom.*) I grabbed a horrible sandwich in the Institute canteen and gobbled it on the way over here.

HELEN
You're always complaining of indigestion.

RALPH
It's nothing. I've got some Rennies. (*He slaps his pockets, and pulls out a small pack of tablets, takes one and sucks it.*)

HELEN
You should see a doctor.

RALPH
Now you're sounding more like a wife than a lover.

HELEN (*gives him a playful slap*)
Go to your meeting.

RALPH (*kisses her*)
I'm gone.

He goes out, followed by HELEN, *seeing him to the front door.*

Music.

Scene Seven

RALPH's *office.* RALPH *comes in and sits down at his desk. He is pensive. He puts his hand on the desk telephone but doesn't dial for a moment. Then he dials. The phone on* HELEN's *desk rings.* HELEN *comes quickly into the room and picks up the phone.*

HELEN
Hello.

RALPH
It's Messenger.

HELEN
Oh. I've been wondering why you hadn't called.

RALPH
Sorry. I've had a lot on my mind.

HELEN
Did Carrie and the children get back all right?

RALPH
Yes, they're fine. But I'm not.

HELEN
What d'you mean?

RALPH
I went to my GP, as you suggested, about the indigestion. I've got a lump on my liver.

HELEN
What kind of lump?

RALPH
He doesn't know. But he couldn't rule out cancer.

HELEN
Oh God!

RALPH
I've got an appointment with a specialist in York on Monday.

HELEN
You poor thing . . . Will I see you before then?

RALPH
Probably not. We'll go to the cottage at the weekend, but Carrie's a bit upset, I think she'd prefer if it was just the family.

HELEN
Of course. I didn't like to phone you earlier, in case –

RALPH
Yes, better not. I'll call you when I can.

HELEN
I love you, Messenger.

She puts down the receiver before he can reply. RALPH *is slightly surprised.*

RALPH
Helen?

He puts down the receiver, then gathers up some papers, puts them in a briefcase and goes out of his office.

HELEN *paces up and down restlessly, then sits down at her laptop and begins to type. She stops and speaks as before.*

HELEN
Why did I say that? I've never said that to him before, not even in the throes of sex, because I was afraid of what it might commit me to. So was it because he might be mortally ill? When I realised I might lose him, I realised I really love him? Or was it the mention of Carrie, the rival woman, which prompted me to say so? In any case, I don't have an equal claim. She is the wife, and the mother. I don't intend to break up their family, even if Messenger wanted to leave her, which I doubt. So what happens when I go back home at the end of the semester? I become a long-distance mistress, snatching a few hours of passion when he has business in London? We make assignations in foreign cities? I see myself sitting in a hotel room with a bottle of champagne in a bucket of melting ice, waiting for him to extricate himself from some conference, and I don't like the picture. (*She resumes typing.*)

Scene Eight

A private hospital room, and HELEN*'s flat.* RALPH, *wearing a hospital theatre robe, dials on his mobile.* HELEN *is typing on her laptop. Her phone rings and she picks it up.*

HELEN
Hello.

RALPH
It's me.

HELEN
Where are you?

RALPH
In hospital, in York. They've kept me in for tests.

HELEN
What did the specialist say?

RALPH
He confirmed I've got a lump on my liver. Doesn't know what it is yet. I've got to have an ultrasound scan and an endoscopy and a colonoscopy.

HELEN
God! What does that entail?

RALPH
Well, a colonoscopy is when they stick a little camera up your rectum and have a look round. It's the medical equivalent of a Channel Five documentary.

HELEN
Poor you.

RALPH
I'm not looking forward to it. You have to go on a diet of tasteless pap for three days beforehand.

HELEN
So you've got to stay in for three days?

RALPH

Yes. Which I can ill afford, with the conference coming up soon.

HELEN

Can I visit you?

RALPH

I think not. (HELEN *is cast down.*) I hate people seeing me in this kind of state.

HELEN

Is Carrie visiting?

RALPH

Well, yes, naturally . . . I couldn't stop her.

HELEN

No.

RALPH

She's been fantastic, actually. Combing the Internet and calling up everybody she knows to find out the best liver man in the country.

HELEN

I wish I could do something . . .

RALPH

There isn't anything.

HELEN

I can't even promise to say a prayer for you, because you would just laugh at me.

RALPH

Well, there's nobody there, is there? But thanks for the thought. (*A knock on his door, off.*) I think it's time for my first test. I'll call you when I have all the results. Bye.

HELEN

Good luck.

RALPH *ends the call. Lights down on* RALPH. HELEN *makes some keystrokes on her laptop and prints out a page. She reads it aloud.*

'She couldn't suppress the feeling that they had brought calamity upon themselves. By giving in to lust, by betraying Carrie – never mind that Carrie had been betraying Messenger in her turn. In her heart, her Catholic heart, she felt that they had sinned, and deserved to be punished. The moment Messenger said, "I've got a lump on my liver," she felt a cold qualm of fear, and yet no surprise – it was as if she had been subconsciously expecting some such blow, and now it had fallen. His lump was probably there before they even met, but telling herself that made no difference. The sin had brought it out, nourished it, made it grow faster. That's what her superstitious self said. She couldn't stop her ears against the silly, hysterical voice, however much she tried. She was in the worst possible plight – to still believe in sin, but no longer in the possibility of absolution.'

She puts down the sheet and resumes typing.

Scene Nine

The hospital room. RALPH, *wearing a hospital robe, is speaking into his recorder.*

RALPH
Two tests down and one to go. I can't complain about the accommodation – private of course. Carrie will spare no expense . . . It's as good as a four-star hotel room, except that you can't hang a 'Do Not Disturb' sign on the doorknob. Nurses are popping in and out all the time to check your pulse or your temperature or your blood pressure or just to ask you if everything is all right . . . They're remarkably good-looking nurses, mind you. Nurse Pomeroy is particularly fetching. She's seen me on television and regards me as something of a celebrity . . . In another mood I might fancy my

chances with Nurse Pomeroy . . . But the fact is
that my libido is on hold at the moment. Ever since
O'Keefe uttered those seven little words, *'You've got
a lump on your liver,'* I've lost interest in sex . . . In
having it, that is. I doubt if you ever stop thinking
about it . . . *I think about sex, therefore I am* . . . If
the lump turns out to be malignant I may never
have sex again. A depressing thought . . . But at
least I can say I went down with guns blazing, with
Helen. Except for the very last time. Pity about
that . . . I've tried to feel the lump myself, but
without success . . . It doesn't hurt . . . which isn't
necessarily a good sign. Cancer of the liver is often
painless in the early stages . . . But it's strange to be
possibly in mortal danger, and not to feel anything
except a little indigestion . . . I read somewhere that
the ancient Assyrians thought the liver was the seat
of the soul. The Egyptians thought it was the heart
and the ancient Greeks the lungs . . . and Descartes
thought his soul was in his pineal gland . . . but the
Assyrians plumped for the liver, though they can't
have had a clue what it was for, physiologically.
Interesting . . .

Knock on door.

> VOICE OF NURSE (*off*)
> Professor Messenger?

> RALPH
> Coming.

He goes out.

Scene Ten

HELEN's *flat. She stands with arms folded, as if looking
abstractedly out of the window. A light on the telephone is
blinking.* HELEN *turns and notices the light. She goes quickly to
press a button on the phone. She listens to a text message*

transmitted in artificial, staccato tones by a male voice, not
RALPH's.

> VOICE MESSAGE
> You have – one – voice message – voice message
> received today at – 3.15 p.m. – Helen — test
> results inconclusive – the specialist wants a – liver
> biopsy – but Carrie has lost faith in him – she has
> fixed an appointment – tomorrow with a man in
> — Harley Street – we are on our way to – London
> – I'll call you when I can – Messenger – end of
> message.

HELEN *listens to this in some distress. She starts to dial a number, but changes her mind and puts the telephone down again.*

Music.

Scene Eleven

The campus. Morning. RALPH, *carrying briefcase, and* HELEN, *carrying an armful of folders, enter from opposite sides, see each other and stop.*

> RALPH
> Hello.

HELEN *comes slowly up to him.*

> HELEN
> I want to drop this stuff and throw my arms around
> you.

> RALPH
> Don't. These buildings have a thousand eyes.

> HELEN
> I know. When did you get back from London?

> RALPH
> Last night.

> HELEN
> And?

RALPH

The news is encouraging. Halib – the Harley Street man – thinks it might be a hydatid cyst. I may have been carrying it about ever since I was a young man.

HELEN

Is it serious?

RALPH

Not life-threatening. It can be surgically removed.

HELEN

But that's wonderful!

RALPH

It is if he's right. I didn't want to call you until I knew for sure.

HELEN

When will that be?

RALPH

Not long. I had a blood test which will tell us.

HELEN

Shouldn't the man in York have thought of that?

RALPH

Yes, he should. Carrie was dead right about him. (*He looks at his watch.*) I've got a meeting, I'm afraid.

HELEN

When will I see you? Alone, I mean.

RALPH

I don't know. Maybe tomorrow afternoon, about five, I could drop by your flat.

HELEN

I've got tutorials tomorrow afternoon, I may be a little late. I'll leave a key in the usual place.

RALPH

OK. (*His mobile rings.*) Excuse me. (*He answers mobile.*) Messenger . . . Yes, Mr Halib. Have you any news? . . . It's positive? Wonderful! Wonderful! . . . I can't thank

you enough . . . Right . . . I'll ring your secretary . . .
Right . . . Thanks again. Goodbye, Mr Halib. (*He turns
to* HELEN.) The test was positive. It *is* a hydatid cyst.

HELEN

Thank God!

RALPH

No, thank Halib.

HELEN

I'm so relieved!

RALPH

So am I. Now I can get on with my life again.

HELEN

I want to kiss you.

RALPH

Better not. Look, I must go, there's a meeting about
the conference . . . I'll see you tomorrow, about five.

HELEN

Right.

They separate and set off in their different directions. RALPH *stops,
takes his mobile out and keys in a memorised number.* HELEN
*stops, turns and observes him a little wistfully, without his being
aware, before going off.*

RALPH

Carrie? I've just had a call from Halib. The test was
positive . . . No, that's *good* news! (*laughs*) It's a cyst
. . . Yes . . . Yes, but they shrink it with drugs before
they operate . . . He's put a prescription in the post
. . . I'm to see him again next week . . .

Fade to black, as he goes off, speaking into his phone.

Yes, he's a genius . . . Thank God you found him
. . . It's a wonderful feeling . . . Yes . . . Yes . . .

Music.

Scene Twelve

HELEN*'s flat and* RALPH*'s office. Day.* HELEN *sits before her laptop, types, stops and speaks, as before.*

> HELEN
> Messenger is coming this afternoon. It will be our first time together since the spectre of cancer reared its ugly head. Now it's been removed, will he want to make love, to celebrate his reprieve? I've been reprieved too, of course, from superstitious fear. But not from an uneasy conscience. Henry James has a fine sentence about illicit love somewhere, in *The Golden Bowl* I think, about how one person's bliss and right can be another person's bale and wrong, like two sides of the same coin. Something like that. I can't deny that our affair was blissful for a while, but the longer it goes on the more likely it is to do harm. Now is the time to end it. I'll tell him this afternoon that we must stop seeing each other, except socially for appearance's sake. Yes, this is the time to do it. My mind is made up. (*Beat.*) Why then, Helen Reed, did you put on your prettiest underwear this morning? Good question.

She switches off her laptop, closes it, and goes out.

RALPH *speaks into his recorder, standing at the window of his office.*

> RALPH
> May the fifth. I'm well, back in control of my life . . . Preparations for the conference are going smoothly . . . All's well at home . . . Carrie and I made love last night for the first time in weeks. This crisis has brought us closer together. At times like this you learn the value of marriage . . . Which leaves only the question of what to do about Helen. I'm standing at the window now, just as I did on that rainy Sunday morning – when was it? – February, and saw her coming round the corner of Biology, and went out to look for her . . . A lot has happened since then . . . The way she said 'I love you' on the phone the other day was a bit alarming, she never said that

before, I hope she isn't getting serious . . . I must be careful when I see her this afternoon . . . she may be planning to make up for lost time . . . I could say, 'I don't feel I'm out of the wood yet, healthwise, let's leave our thing on hold until I'm really well again.' Then soon I'll be fully occupied with the conference, and not long after that the semester will end and she'll be going back to London and the affair can die a natural death. Perhaps one last fuck for old times' sake if she's up for it . . . But not today. Not today.

He switches off the recorder with a certain emphasis, as if concluding the audio journal, puts it in his desk drawer, locks the drawer, then goes out.

Scene Thirteen

HELEN*'s flat. It is unoccupied. The doorbell chimes. After an interval, the sound of the front door opening and shutting, and* RALPH *comes into the room, a latchkey in his hand. He looks around the room, and puts the key down on the table, next to the closed laptop. His gaze lingers on the laptop, and he runs his fingers over the lid. He sits down on the armchair, but continues to gaze thoughtfully at the laptop. He checks the time on his wristwatch, gazes again at the laptop. Suddenly he gets to his feet, goes across to the desk, sits down and opens the laptop. Hastily, furtively, he boots up the computer and uses the mouse to access a file. He looks up, and pricks his ears for any sound of* HELEN *returning. He checks his watch again, and begins to scroll through the file, smiling occasionally. Then suddenly he reads something that shocks him. He stares incredulously at the screen.*

> RALPH
> Carrie?

The sound of the front door opening and shutting. RALPH *gives a start, hastily turns off the computer and closes it.*

> HELEN (*off*)
> Messenger – are you here?

Act Two Scene Thirteen

RALPH *gets up and moves away from the desk just as* HELEN *comes into the room.*

> HELEN (*smiles*)
> Oh, there you are. (*He is unable to disguise his perturbation.*) What's the matter?

> RALPH
> Who is Carrie having an affair with?

HELEN *freezes.*

Pause.

> HELEN
> I don't know.

> RALPH
> Why didn't you tell me?

> HELEN
> She told me in confidence.

> RALPH
> So it's not some fantasy of yours, some scenario for one of your novels?

> HELEN
> What d'you mean, scenario? How did you find out?

RALPH *glances at the computer.* HELEN *follows his glance.*

> HELEN
> You've been reading my journal!

> RALPH
> Yes.

> HELEN
> I can't believe it.

> RALPH
> I'm sorry.

> HELEN
> It's despicable.

74

RALPH
Yes, it is.

HELEN
It's despicable and inexcusable and unforgivable.
How could you do such a thing?

RALPH
I couldn't stop myself. You have no idea who she's
fucking?

HELEN
No, and now I'd be grateful if you would go away
and leave me alone.

RALPH
When I find out I'll beat the shit out of him.

HELEN
Do you really think you have the right?

RALPH *cannot think of a reply.*

HELEN
If I were you I wouldn't confront Carrie.

RALPH
Why not?

HELEN
She's well aware of what *you* get up to, when you're
away from home.

RALPH
What d'you mean?

HELEN
She told me. She has plenty of evidence.

RALPH
What evidence?

HELEN
Letters, hotel bills, in your pockets. Lipstick.

RALPH
Lipstick?

HELEN

On a shirt – not Carrie's shade. You've been very careless. Once she found a tape recording of you in bed with someone who was having a very noisy orgasm.

RALPH

Jesus. (*He is racked with conflicting impulses – fight or flight? Defend himself or grovel? And to which woman?*) I can explain that.

HELEN

I'm not interested.

RALPH

I mean to Carrie. It was just a one-night stand. It meant nothing.

HELEN

And our affair – did that mean nothing?

RALPH

No, of course not . . . (*defeated*) What a mess.

HELEN

Would you go now?

RALPH

Helen – I hope we can still be friends.

HELEN

I don't think so.

RALPH

But Carrie will notice! She'll wonder why.

HELEN

That's your problem. Please go.

RALPH (*goes to leave, then turns*)

You will still do the Last Word, won't you? It's been announced.

HELEN (*contemptuous*)

Yes, I'll do it.

RALPH
Thank you.

RALPH *leaves.* HELEN *sits down and sobs.*

Fade to black. Music.

Scene Fourteen

HELEN *is standing at a lectern in a spotlight, against a dark background, with a screen or screens behind and above her, delivering her talk. Her open laptop is within reach.*

HELEN
... and so, before I came to this university, and
visited the Institute, I wasn't even aware that
scientists were concerned with consciousness.
Now at least I understand their interest. In a way
it's the most fascinating subject of all, because
it's an investigation into what makes us human.
Understanding consciousness, it occurred to me
this weekend, is to modern science what the quest
for the Philosopher's Stone was to alchemy. The
substance that would turn base metal into gold
was never found, but the search for it led to many
genuine discoveries in chemistry. Perhaps we shall
never fully understand consciousness, but the
effort to do so has already yielded many fascinating
discoveries about the brain and the mind, some
of which have been described to us over the past
three days. No speaker, however, has made any
reference to literature. This I find surprising,
because literature is a written record of human
consciousness, arguably the richest we have. Let
me give you an example – a poem called the 'The
Garden', by the seventeenth-century English poet,
Andrew Marvell. One of its stanzas describes the
sensuous pleasures of an ideal garden.

She touches her keyboard, checks that the stanza has appeared on the screen, and then recites the words which she knows by heart.

Act Two Scene Fourteen

What wond'rous Life in this I lead!
Ripe Apples drop about my head;
The Luscious Clusters of the Vine
Upon my Mouth do crush their Wine;
The Nectaren, and curious Peach,
Into my hands themselves do reach;
Stumbling on Melons, as I pass,
Insnar'd with Flow'rs, I fall on Grass.

We've heard a lot about qualia in the last three
days. There is division of opinion, I understand,
about whether or not they are first-person
phenomena forever inaccessible to the third-person
discourse of science. I am not competent to
adjudicate on this issue. But let me point to a
paradox about Marvell's verse, which applies to
lyric poetry in general. Although he speaks in the
first person, Marvell does not speak for himself
alone. In reading this stanza we enhance our own
experience of the qualia of fruit and fruitfulness.
We see the fruit, we taste it and smell it and savour
it with what has been called 'the thrill of
recognition' and yet it is not there, it is the virtual
reality of fruit, conjured up by the qualia of the
poem itself, its subtle and unique combination of
sounds and rhythms and meanings which I could
try to analyse if there were world enough and time,
to quote another poem of Marvell's, but there is
not.

'The Garden' is a celebratory poem, it focuses on
consciousness as a state of happiness. It is about
bliss. But there is a tragic dimension to
consciousness, which has also not been mentioned
in this conference. There is depression, madness,
guilt and dread. There is the fear of death – and
strangest of all, the fear of life. If human beings are
the only living creatures that know they are going
to die, they are also the only ones who take their
own lives. For some people, in some circumstances,
consciousness becomes so unbearable that they

commit suicide to bring it to an end. 'To be or not to be?' is a peculiarly human question. Literature can help us to understand the dark side of consciousness too.

Later in the poem, Marvell compares his soul to a bird, and imagines it leaving his body temporarily to perch on the branch of a tree, preening itself in anticipation of its final flight to heaven. I don't expect to carry you with him there. But the Christian idea of the soul is continuous with the humanist idea of the self – that is to say, personal identity, the sense of one's mental and emotional life having a unity and an ethical responsibility, sometimes called conscience.

That idea of the self is under attack today, not only in science but in the humanities too. We are told that it is a fiction, an illusion, a myth. That each of us is 'just a pack of neurons', or just a junction for converging discourses, or just a parallel processing computer running by itself without an operator. As a human being and as a writer, I find that view of consciousness abhorrent – and intuitively unconvincing. I want to hold on to the traditional idea of the autonomous individual self. A lot that we value in civilisation seems to depend on it.

Thank you.

Sound of applause, which HELEN *acknowledges with a polite smile and a nod of the head, gradually changing to noise of an audience leaving an auditorium with a buzz of conversation.* HELEN *gathers up her papers, puts them in a document case and disappears into the darkness behind her.*

Scene Fifteen

The campus. HELEN *carrying her document case.* RALPH *enters, pursuing her.*

RALPH
Helen!

HELEN *stops and waits for him to approach her.*

RALPH
Helen, congratulations. That was great. Exactly what I was hoping for.

HELEN
But you don't believe a word of it.

RALPH
No. But you expressed the ideas so beautifully. They were spellbound.

HELEN
There was a man asleep in the front row.

RALPH
He probably spent too much time in the bar last night. You could tell from the applause how much it was appreciated.

HELEN
I'm glad you think so.

RALPH
I was really impressed by how well you've grasped the issues – and even the jargon.

HELEN
Well, you're a good teacher, Ralph Messenger, whatever your failings in other respects. (*She makes to go.*)

RALPH
And I was very struck by what you said about the dark side of consciousness. About some people finding it unbearable.

HELEN
Yes.

RALPH (*hesitantly*)
Did you . . . have you ever . . . ?

HELEN
Oh, don't worry – I'm not going to top myself on
account of you.

RALPH
I didn't mean that! But something about the way you
spoke . . . it seemed very personal.

HELEN *is silent for a moment, wondering whether to respond.*
RALPH *waits.*

HELEN
I *am* prone to depression – many writers are. It's almost
an occupational disease. And once, it was so bad that
I really didn't want to go on living. But I could never
take my own life. It's probably the last remnant of my
Catholic faith – that despair is the unforgivable sin.

RALPH
I don't have that problem. When I thought I might
have cancer, I decided that if it was confirmed and
the condition was incurable, I wouldn't hang around
and die by inches. I found making that decision was a
great comfort.

HELEN
Well, that's one of many differences between us.
But at least I've finished grieving for Martin now. I
suppose I owe that to you.

RALPH
I'm glad.

HELEN
Goodbye, Messenger. (*She turns to leave.*)

RALPH
You're leaving soon?

HELEN
Tomorrow morning.

RALPH
Ah. So what are you going to do when you get back
to London?

Act Two Scene Fifteen

HELEN

Start a new novel.

RALPH

Excellent! You've got an idea?

HELEN

And a title. *Crying is a Puzzler.*

RALPH

Crying is a Puzzler. What's it about?

HELEN

You'll have to wait and see, won't you? Goodbye.

She goes off, leaving RALPH *gazing uncertainly after her.*

RALPH

Goodbye, Helen.

Fade to black. Music.

David Lodge's novels include *Changing Places*, *Small World*, *Nice Work*, *Author, Author*, *Deaf Sentence* and, most recently, *A Man of Parts*. He has also written stage plays and screenplays, and several works of literary criticism, including *The Art of Fiction*, *Consciousness and the Novel* and *The Year of Henry James*.